The West Coast Murders

Roy MacGregor

An M&S Paperback Original from
McClelland & Stewart Inc.
The Canadian Publishers

For Shannon and Katie Hall, and for all the summers
at Camp Lake.

The author is grateful to Doug Gibson, who thought up this series,
and to Alex Schultz, who pulls it off.

An M&S Paperback Original from
McClelland & Stewart Ltd.

National Library of Canada Cataloguing in Publication

MacGregor, Roy, 1948 –
    The West coast murders

(The Screech Owls series; 12)
ISBN 0-7710-5623-0

I. Title.   II. Series: MacGregor, Roy, 1948 –
Screech Owls series; 12.

PS8575.G84W47 2000   jC813'.54   C00-930695-1
PZ7.M333We 2000

We acknowledge the financial support of the Government of Canada
through the Book Publishing Industry Development Program and
that of the Government of Ontario through the Ontario Media
Development Corporation's Ontario Book Initiative. We further
acknowledge the support of the Canada Council for the Arts and the
Ontario Arts Council for our publishing program.

Cover illustration by Gregory C. Banning
Typeset in Bembo by M&S, Toronto

Printed and bound in Canada

McClelland & Stewart Ltd.
The Canadian Publishers
481 University Avenue
Toronto, Ontario
M5G 2E9
www.mcclelland.com

3 4 5 6   06 05 04

1

IT WAS SARAH WHO SPOTTED THE FIRST BODY.

She was standing high on the bridge of the Zodiac, staring out over the rolling sea off the San Juan Islands.

Travis had seen her get to her feet and point, but with the wind roaring in his ears he couldn't hear what she had shouted to the guide on the tour boat. Whatever it was, it caused the guide to stand, draw her binoculars up, and stare in the direction Sarah was pointing for some time before suddenly turning the Zodiac and revving the engines.

The big open tour boat headed towards the area where Sarah was still pointing. The swells were high along the Strait of Juan de Fuca this early in the year, and at times the islands dropped out of sight for a moment before the Zodiac roared up the next wide, rolling wave.

Travis didn't mind the rolling. The same, unfortunately, could not be said for Nish, who lay flat on the floor of the Whale Watch tour boat and had turned the oddest colour of green Travis had ever seen in a human face.

This was not the Nish they had started out with from Victoria Harbour. Before the Zodiac had rounded the breakwater and headed out into open sea, Nish had bounced about the big rubber-sided boat like a tropical storm – "Hurricane Nish," Sarah had tagged him – and soon had everyone on the tour, Muck and Mr. Dillinger, all the Screech Owls, even the guide, howling with laughter as he kept interrupting the guide's talk about where they'd be going and what they'd be seeing.

They would be watching for dolphins and porpoises, the guide told them, and with luck they might even see a massive grey whale. She explained how to tell the porpoises from the dolphins. She told them there were more than thirty different kinds of dolphins in the world, and how it was important to protect them.

"Not long ago we were losing twenty thousand of them a year in gill nets," the guide said. "Tuna fishermen were letting them get tangled in the nets they were using to catch tuna, and the dolphins were drowning. Like us, they need to breathe air. We've saved a lot of them, but it still happens. That's why all the dolphins we find off the coast of British Columbia are protected by law; we don't want anybody, or anything, hurting them.

"Everyone knows they're mammals, of course, not fish. They're as intelligent as chimpanzees and have memories like elephants. They're better with numbers and better at following complicated instructions than most of us are – so treat them with respect. They may be smarter than us."

"Certainly smarter than *some* of us," Sarah added, with a withering look at Nish.

Nish crossed his eyes and rolled his tongue before sticking it out at Sarah and violently shaking his head.

The guide said any dolphins they saw today would likely be Pacific white-sided dolphins, which were common along this coast. Killer whales, she added, were also dolphins and could be found off the coast of British Columbia as well, though they are rarely seen. They might get lucky, but more likely they'd see a big grey, which was just as good, in her opinion.

"Greys are beautiful animals," she said. "Some of them are longer than a city bus, and once they get here they spend most of their time eating tiny little sea creatures they find in these waters. An adult grey will eat about twelve hundred kilograms of food a day – that's the equivalent of ten thousand Big Macs."

"*That's what I usually order!*" Nish had shouted.

The dolphins, the guide said, prefer salmon, but also love a good feed of anchovies.

"*They order pizza out here, with anchovies?*" Nish had screeched. "*I think I'm gonna hurl!*"

And less than ten minutes later, with the sea rolling and sliding and slipping under him, he had indeed "hurled," a small figure in a rain suit and life jacket hanging over the back of the Zodiac and barfing into the open sea as seagulls screeched overhead and the rest of the Owls mercilessly applauded and cheered his every retch.

Now Nish was flat out, green and groaning – but at least he was quiet. This was no time for wisecracks. Whatever Sarah had sighted, it seemed to have the guide deeply concerned.

Twice they turned and circled back, the guide continually rising from her pilot's chair to lift the binoculars and scan the rolling sea for whatever it was that Sarah had seen.

"*There!*" Sarah called, pointing. This time Travis heard her.

The guide turned the Zodiac sharply, easing it up one long, rolling swell and down the other side, where, almost magically, the boat drew up alongside the object of their search mission.

Travis, sitting on an outside seat beside Sam, Nish's new partner on defence, leaned over the round rubbery wall of the Zodiac and stared hard.

It was a dolphin – rolling lifelessly in the sea, shreds of pale, white flesh stringing out in the water from its underside.

And something else – fading to pink in the water, but dark red closer to the rolling, unreal looking dolphin.

Blood.

"I think *I'm* gonna hurl," said Sam in her deepest voice.

"What happened?" Travis asked.

"Maybe it got struck by a ship?" suggested Data, who was strapped into a seat just the other side of Sam.

The guide was out of her pilot's seat and down close to the side of the Zodiac. She had out a long pole with a hook on the end and reached with it into the water. But the boat was rolling too much. Muck, the Screech Owls' coach, stood to help. "You take the controls," he said to her. "I'll pull it in."

The guide nodded, and a moment later she had put the outboard engines into reverse and pulled the boat around so that it and the dolphin were at least drifting in the same direction.

Muck, his lips tight and jaw set, reached for the dolphin with the pole and caught it along a front flipper, the hook pulling the creature so it rolled over completely as it came towards the Zodiac.

There was a black, gaping hole on the dolphin's other side, fresh blood still streaming from the wound.

The guide came down from her seat for a closer look. "What the –?" she said.

"A swordfish?" Data suggested. "Ran it right through?"

Muck was shaking his head. "I don't think so," he said. "It's been shot."

2

IT WAS TRAVIS WHO SPOTTED THE SECOND BODY.

Muck and Mr. Dillinger had tried to hoist the dead dolphin into the Zodiac, but it was too large and slippery for them to handle, so they ended up using the mooring ropes to lash the poor creature to the side of the boat while the guide made slowly for harbour.

All of the Screech Owls were upset. They'd come out to see grey whales swimming and playing in the sea, and they'd found, instead, a dead dolphin. "Shot," Muck had said, but it made no sense to Travis. Shot for what reason? he wondered. And who would do such a thing?

Jenny Staples, the Owls' goalie, was sobbing. A few of the others, Fahd included, were brushing away tears and trying to pretend that it was just the splash from the sea. Travis's throat felt tight and he avoided having to talk. He sat, staring at the rolling horizon, and tried to think of anything but the death of this beautiful creature that now lay strapped to the side of the boat, blood stringing out pink behind the small wake that rippled from its tail fin.

6

Muck and Mr. Dillinger talked in low voices as they leaned over the side making sure their ties held. The coach said it must have something to do with tuna fishermen and gill nets, but Mr. Dillinger didn't think there was any tuna fishing done off these waters. Mr. Dillinger said it must have been some idiot with a rifle out for nothing more than a kick, but Muck shook his head in disgust. Muck looked angry, as if somehow this attack on an innocent sea creature had been an attack on himself and his team of peewee players.

On the slow journey back to shore, a huge, mottled grey whale breached off to one side. The next time the gigantic dark creature rose out of the water, several of the Owls raised their disposable cameras and clicked off a few shots before it disappeared again in a thundering crash of spray, but they did so without much enthusiasm. Hardly anyone said a word, except to point out where the whale was coming up again.

Soon, however, it had moved off and there was only the slow drone of the engines on low speed, the trickling sound of water as it played between the trussed dolphin and the side of the boat, and the hypnotic rise and fall, rise and fall of the wide, rolling sea.

Some of the Owls were dozing off. Fahd was slumped over. Sarah was leaning on Sam, both of them nodding sharply from time to time as they bobbed in and out of sleep. Andy lay against

Wilson in the seats up ahead. Dmitri and Lars and Simon were asleep too, their hooded heads down low as if in prayer.

Travis kept watching the sea. He could not stop wondering how this had happened. If Muck was right and the dolphin had been shot, could it really have been for *sport*? For a *kick*? Maybe it was a fisherman who'd accidentally caught the dolphin in his nets, and when he couldn't untangle the poor creature he had put it out of its misery.

But that didn't seem possible. There was no torn netting on the dolphin, just the gaping black hole in one side where dark blood was still seeping out and thinning to pink, eventually fading to nothing as it washed away in the sea.

Perhaps the dolphin hadn't been shot. Maybe Muck was wrong. Maybe it was a shark attack! A swordfish, like Fahd said. A bite from some fierce sea creature. Maybe it was the mark of a suction cup from the arm of a giant squid or octopus.

But Travis knew nothing about the ocean and decided he shouldn't pretend to. He'd have to wait, like everyone else, to find out what had happened. He just hoped it wasn't a gun that had done this.

Would it be murder? he wondered. Can you *murder* a dolphin? Or does it have to be a human before it counts for that much. But then the guide had said they're smart as us, they breathe like us, they can learn, they speak to each other.

It would be murder in Travis Lindsay's opinion, anyway.

He tried to doze off, but couldn't. He watched, instead, the slowly approaching land and the islands merging into the horizon behind. It was difficult adjusting to the size of the ocean after all those summers at his grandparents' little lake up near Algonquin Park, where he and Nish last summer had managed to swim from shore to shore while Travis's dad stayed alongside in the rowboat and kept a sharp eye out for waterskiers and wakeboarders. At the lake he was never out of sight of the shore. Here, if he looked to his left – what had the guide called it, port? – he could see nothing. For all he knew, there *was* nothing in that direction all the way to Japan.

He was staring out, thinking of Japan and Nagano and the Big Hat arena, when suddenly he thought he saw something. He half stood, but then crouched back down. He didn't want to shout out if it was nothing. Maybe it was just his imagination playing tricks on him.

He waited for the next long roll of the sea. Then he saw it again – a flash of something white.

Another dolphin?

He waited until he had seen it twice more before he said anything. By now he was sure. He stepped over to the pilot's seat, where the guide was nursing the controls and staring ahead towards her destination.

When Travis finally caught her eye, she looked down, wary. It occurred to Travis that she, too, might have been crying.

He pointed to the west. His voice caught slightly. "I-I see something over that way."

The guide said nothing. She stood up, raised her binoculars, and stared for a long time. One long swell, then a second, then a third, the guide still staring, seemingly as uncertain as Travis had been.

She put the glasses down, and Travis saw a look of extreme anger flash across her face. She said nothing to him, but turned back towards the two men on the far side still holding the dolphin tight to the Zodiac.

"We have another sighting on the port side!" she called.

Muck and Mr. Dillinger looked up, Mr. Dillinger's eyes blinking behind water-spotted glasses. "Of what?" he called.

"I don't know," said the guide. "I'm not sure."

Muck got to his feet, lifted his hand to shield his eyes, and stared. "We'd better check it out."

The guide said nothing. She turned the boat at once towards the object Travis had seen. The movement jolted the dozing Screech Owls and several stirred. Sam and Sarah stood up together, staring out to see where they were going.

"W-wh-what's goin' on?" said a voice below Travis. He stared down into a face that was not nearly as green as it had been a half-hour earlier. Still, Nish did not look at all well.

"We're turning," Travis said. "There's something in the water."

"*Fish?*" Nish said sarcastically.

Nish was trying to smile. He was coming back, recovering from his bout of seasickness.

"You want to sit up?" Travis asked.

"Give me a hand."

Travis helped his pal onto the seat beside him. Nish shook his head and rubbed his face.

Slowly, at times almost seeming to go backwards, the Zodiac crawled over the rolling swells towards whatever was floating in the distance.

Most of the Owls were awake by now and knew they were headed for something in the water. Sarah and Sam were trying to stand in order to see better, but with the rolling waves and slippery floor of the Zodiac, it wasn't easy. They plunked down and waited like everyone else.

Travis could feel the tension rise around him. The white thing he had first seen in the distance was drawing closer, visible now with each swell rather than just every so often. From time to time the guide lifted her binoculars to check. Her concern seemed to be growing. ·

She pulled the Zodiac around to starboard, then hard left again to port. The Zodiac rose up and over a wave, and then slipped down into the same trough of sea that held the mystery object.

Travis and Nish both moved to the side of the boat, staring hard.

It was a white shirt, drifting slowly in the water.

And from inside the shirt came a familiar dark stain, fading to pink, just as it had around the dolphin.

The object rolled easily in the waves, tumbling to reveal a gaping black hole in the white cloth almost exactly the same as the wound on the dolphin.

Only this was a man!

Travis turned in shock to Nish.

Nish had gone green. He looked like he was about to be sick all over again. But he was pointing, his finger shaking.

"What?" Travis asked impatiently.

"*W-we . . . know . . . him!*"

3

TWO DAYS EARLIER THE SCREECH OWLS HAD BEEN in a plane over the Rocky Mountains. The snow-covered peaks of the higher summits, poking up through a soft mattress of cloud, were the only reminder of the winter they had left behind.

In Vancouver, their destination, it was more like early summer. On the long ride in from the airport, they were thrilled to see pink cherry trees, red and yellow tulips, gardens like living rainbows with everything in full bloom.

Rarely had the Screech Owls looked forward to a trip so much. It was not just that this was beautiful British Columbia, with everything from the mountains to the ocean; they'd also be playing in a totally new kind of hockey tournament. Vancouver was hosting the first-ever "3-on-3" International Peewee Competition. Several of the matches were to be played in nearby Bellingham, Washington, just across the Canada–U.S. border, which would give the tournament a genuine *international* flavour. Teams from all over North America had been invited – from Quebec City to Anaheim, from Winnipeg to New York City – but they were not going to compete as teams. Instead, each team would be split into groups of three skaters – usually two forwards and a defence – which would compete in different divisions for separate championship trophies.

It was an idea that Wayne Gretzky and other hockey leaders came up with when they met to talk about what was right and what was wrong in minor hockey. A great many of the top National Hockey League stars these days came from Europe, even though far more people played hockey in Canada and the United States. So what was their secret?

Wayne Gretzky and the others came up with a number of suggestions. First – and much to the disgust of Nish – Canadian and American minor hockey teams needed to practise more and play fewer games and tournaments. "*Gimme a break!*" Nish had howled. "*That's like choosing school over summer vacation!*"

But another idea sounded more attractive. What about bringing shinny back into the organized game? Gretzky said he'd learned his skills in his backyard, not through organized practices where he couldn't work on the tricks that would make him the greatest player of all time.

Perhaps "3-on-3" hockey should become part of the organized game. In Europe, where they play on a larger ice surface, they had been playing

3-on-3 for decades, using the width of the ice rather than the length. They could, by dividing the rink at the bluelines, run three games of 3-on-3 at the same time.

In Canada, a group of former NHLers was now building smaller 3-on-3 rinks around the country, and the game was catching on with everyone from little kids to old men. The first rinks had been built around Vancouver, and so this was where the idea for the first international 3-on-3 shinny tournament had taken root.

To the Screech Owls' great surprise, Muck Munro had been enthusiastic about the tournament. He believed in tradition, and didn't much care for newfangled ideas. But for Muck, shinny was not a new idea. And when the Owls remembered the joy in Muck's face when Tamarack froze over and he'd come out to play on the frozen fields, they understood why he was all for this "new" idea of bringing fun and creativity back into the game.

Each group would, of course, also have a goaltender, but Jeremy Weathers and Jenny Staples would split those duties. The hard part was figuring out who would play with whom, and some of Muck's combinations were surprising.

One Monday evening after practice, he pinned a notice to the bulletin board in the Owls' dressing room:

Screech Owls 3-on-3 Teams

Elite Division

Team 1: Sarah Cuthbertson – Travis Lindsay
– Wayne Nishikawa

Team 2: Dmitri Yakushev – Andy Higgins –
Lars Johansson

Canucks Division

Team 3: Fahd Noorizadeh – Gordie Griffith
– Samantha Bennett

Rockies Division

Team 4: Liz Moscovitz – Derek Dillinger –
Willie Granger

Pacific Division

Team 5: Simon Milliken – Jesse Highboy –
Wilson Kelly

"*Not Sarah!*" Nish shouted as he leaned over
Travis's shoulder, reading Muck's list. "*Why is she
on my team? Why me? Why me?*"

Travis just shook his head. He knew Muck's
decision was a good one. Nish and Sarah actually
played wonderfully together, even if sometimes
it seemed they were more interested in taking
shots at each other than at the opposing goaltender. Travis was delighted to be included on
the first team with them.

Muck had done a splendid job. He'd entered two 3-on-3 groups in the toughest division, and had spread the Owls' talent evenly through the other divisions. Travis could sense how disappointed Sam was not to be included on one of the top two lines, but with only one defender in each group, what else could Muck do? Nish was, well, Nish, and he always came through. And Lars had grown up playing 3-on-3 in Sweden and was probably the best shinny player of them all.

From Christmas on, the excitement built. The Owls still played in their league, but sometimes they could think of little but the upcoming tournament. They practised hard, spending the last twenty minutes of every session on 3-on-3 shinny, just getting used to each other and trying tricks they wouldn't dare attempt in a real league game.

The tournament was scheduled for the Easter long weekend, and an extra day was being added at each end, giving them nearly a week in Vancouver for the tournament and plenty of time for sightseeing.

"*Wreck Beach!*" Nish announced. "That's the only thing I want to see."

"What's Wreck Beach?" Fahd asked.

Nish looked at Fahd as if he had just crawled out of an old hockey bag and had never before seen the real world.

"*Are you serious?*" Nish asked. "It's the *nude* beach. I'm going as soon as we get there."

"You'll freeze," said Sarah.

"Come and see for yourself," Nish challenged.

"We will," said Sarah.

"And we'll be bringing cameras," laughed Sam. "*With telephoto lenses!*"

"Very funny," Nish sneered. "*Very, very funny.*"

So far, however, they hadn't come within a mile of Wreck Beach, wherever that was (How does Nish find out about these things? wondered Travis), but they had all walked across the famous Capilano rope bridge, which hangs, and swings, high above a gorge. All, that is, but Nish, who stayed in the van claiming he had food poisoning when, in fact, he was just terrified of heights. They saw the steam-powered clock in Gastown, the harbour, they walked around Stanley Park, and had a wonderful time at the Vancouver Aquarium.

Sarah and Sam were particularly keen on the Aquarium. They had wanted to see the killer whales – a baby had just been born – and all the Owls were fascinated by the special tour the staff put on for them.

They were allowed to feed the sea lions. Sarah and Sam were kissed by a killer whale. They saw the penguins, and when Fahd said how much one chubby, preening penguin in the corner looked like Nish even the staff laughed at the red-faced exhibitionist. They heard a lecture on dolphins and porpoises and grey whales, and one of the attendants, Brad, even took them into the research area and showed them how the dolphins could talk to each other and how, in a matter of a few minutes, he could teach them a new trick.

It had been, until now, the most riveting moment of the trip.

"W-we . . . know . . . him!"

The urgency in Nish's voice was real. He wasn't kidding. He was dead serious, and terrified.

Travis turned back from his friend and stared into the water just in time to see the head roll around again, eyes open and blank and very, very dead, the mouth twisted in pain that could no longer be felt.

"IT'S BRAD!"

The scream came from Sam, pushing hard against Travis's shoulder.

"OH MY GOD!"

That was Sarah. She was already bursting into sobs.

Travis forced himself to look again when the body rolled over once more. It *was* Brad, the marine biologist from the Vancouver Aquarium.

Brad, who had taken them to see the dolphins.

Brad, who had so charmed Sarah and Sam.

Brad, with a gaping black wound in his chest that matched the wound on the dolphin now strapped to the side of the Zodiac.

4

TRAVIS WAS GRATEFUL THAT MUCK AND MR. Dillinger had come out whale watching with the team. The two men had taken care of the dolphin, and now they quickly took charge again. Muck ordered the Screech Owls to look in the other direction, which they did; not even intense curiosity could cause Travis to turn around. Nor did Nish turn, proof that the one thing more frightening than anything he could imagine was at that moment being lifted up out of the sea by Muck and Mr. Dillinger and hauled into the Zodiac.

When Travis finally did look, the body had been covered by a plastic tarpaulin and Mr. Dillinger was tying down the ends, making sure the wind blew nothing free. Muck went back to hold tight to the strapped dolphin, and the guide turned the boat, once again, towards shore.

No one said a word the whole way in to Victoria Harbour. The guide had obviously radioed ahead, because there were police cars with lights flashing and an ambulance and first-aid workers waiting for their arrival. They must have known it was a dead body coming in – two, if they counted the dolphin – so Travis figured the first-aid people could be there for only one reason: the Screech Owls.

But the Owls all seemed to handle it well. There were some sobs, of course. And Travis could see Fahd shaking and pretending it was because of the cold. But Mr. Dillinger and Muck's quick thinking meant the shock was not as bad as it might have been. The first-aid workers talked to them all and checked them over, and Nish was given a Gravol for his still-churning stomach. Everyone else was fine – at least physically.

A windowless van from the Aquarium took away the carcass of the dolphin, and a special police vehicle showed up to cart the body of the marine biologist away to the morgue.

The police interviewed the guide and Muck and Mr. Dillinger, and after they'd all signed statements and given their addresses and telephone numbers while staying in Vancouver, the police told the Screech Owls they were free to go.

"Why wouldn't they interview me?" Nish whined as the last of the police cars pulled out. "I'm the one who identified the body."

"Perhaps you could tell them how he was killed, too," said Sam with more than a touch of sarcasm. Her eyes were red from crying.

"Obviously," protested Nish, "he was shot."

"By *who?*" Sarah asked. "And *why?*"

"You expect me to know *everything*?"

"You always act like you do."

But not this time, Travis thought. No one knew.

Why had there been a dolphin out there floating dead, a gaping black hole in its side?

And why a short distance away a man – a man who knew everything there was to know about dolphins – obviously murdered?

Mr. Dillinger was wonderful on the way back to Vancouver. He cranked up the rock music on the old bus the organizers had made available to the various teams, and once they were on the ferry he got change for a hundred-dollar bill and walked around handing out money so the Owls could lose themselves and their thoughts in chips and gravy and video games.

Nish, now fully recovered from his seasickness, was intent on winning a wristwatch from a machine that required him to work a crane with a metal grab over the desired object, drop it down, snatch the prize and then drop it into a chute. So far he'd won three "prizes": a key chain, a pair of ruby-red plastic lips, and a badly stitched, stuffed doll. He hadn't even come close to the watch.

Travis left his pal pumping in quarters and cursing the fates, and went out on the deck for a walk around the big ferry. The wind felt fresh on his face. The sun was out, a spring sun burning like summer, and he thought he'd walk back towards the stern of the boat – "The *poop* deck!" Nish had happily shouted when one of the deckhands asked the Owls if they knew any of the names for the parts of a ship – and watch the gulls swirl above the wake.

Travis hoped Nish left his brain to science when he died. It was worth taking a closer look at the mind of a twelve-year-old whose great ambition in life was to find a nude beach. Of course, they'd have to scrub it down before touching it.

The ferry was just crossing a narrows between two large islands. It was such a beautiful sight, the leaves already out, the trees and bushes in bloom, the hills in the distance and rocky shoreline so near. He could see a farmhouse on one side, and wondered what it was like to live there and be able to look out one window and see horses grazing and out the other and see a huge ferry filled with people and cars and trucks churning by, everyone on deck trying to stare in at you and see what you look like.

There were others out on the deck. An old couple, just standing at the rail and staring, their arms linked. A student sitting up beside one of the vents, an open book on her lap with the pages flipping in the wind. And down towards the stern, Nish's "poop deck," he could make out a couple of Screech Owls windbreakers.

Their backs were turned to Travis, but he knew who it was. The flying, waving light brown hair was obviously Sarah. And the carrot top bouncing wildly in the wind was Sam.

The noise was extraordinary. He could hear the big engines churning and pounding. He could hear the bubbling roar that came up from the big propellers.

"*Hey!*" he called out over the noise.

Travis wasn't sure exactly what he saw next. A quick motion by Sam. Sarah hunching her shoulders as if she was trying to hide herself in her windbreaker. Something spinning out into the wake. Perhaps it was only a gull twisting down.

Sarah turned, sheepishly. "Hey, Trav – how's it going?"

"Okay – what's up?"

"Nothin'," Sarah said. He couldn't help but notice the high colour in her cheeks. It couldn't be from the sun; the clouds had parted only half an hour before.

Sam was breathing out, hard, her lips so tightly pursed it looked like she was whistling. Only instead of a shrill whistle coming out, there was a steady, thin flow of steam. Like winter breath in Tamarack – only here it wasn't cold.

It wasn't steam, it was smoke!

Travis tried to think of something to say but found he couldn't.

"You guys see Lars?" he asked instead. He hadn't even been thinking of Lars up to this moment.

Sarah seemed relieved. She smiled, flushing even deeper. "I saw him earlier. I think he's on the upper deck."

Sam said nothing. She was looking warily at Travis, as if trying to figure out how much he'd seen.

"Okay," Travis found himself saying. "Thanks. See you later."

He was gone before they said anything, gone in one quick turn, and was soon bounding up the stairs in search of time to think, not looking for Lars at all.

What was happening here?

Bodies in the water?

Murder?

Sarah Cuthbertson smoking?

This latest development was almost as upsetting.

Sarah Cuthbertson smoking?

5

"I *WASN'T* SMOKING, TRAVIS. I SWEAR!"

Sarah spoke in a whisper, but it may as well have been a shout the way her pained voice cut through the small dressing room. She was hurt, and it showed in her eyes and sounded in her voice.

Sarah hadn't denied that Sam was smoking. She said Sam had bummed the smoke off another passenger, an older teenager. This older girl had even offered Sarah one and just shrugged when Sarah refused. Sam had taken the second one and had smoked them both.

"Sam was upset about what we'd seen," Sarah said. "That was all."

"Muck would suspend her if he knew," Travis said. "Besides, she shouldn't smoke."

It rattled Travis to think that a teammate – someone exactly the same age as he was – would be smoking. And not one cigarette as an experiment, but a second, almost as if she *needed* it.

"He'd have kicked you off the team, too," Travis thought to add.

Sarah looked on the verge of tears. "I was just *standing* with her," she protested.

"You didn't stop her."

Sarah was frustrated. "I'm not her mother!"

"You're her teammate," Travis said. "You both have a responsibility to the Owls."

Inside, Travis winced. It was he who sounded like someone's mother. But he was captain, wasn't he? He was supposed to set an example. And if he saw something that wasn't right, he had to say so. Either that or go to Muck.

Any further discussion on the matter was over when a large rear end came through the door. It was Nish, in full gear except for skates, pushing the door open with his butt while he made sure his freshly sharpened blades didn't nick up against the door frame.

Right behind Nish – well, technically, right in *front* of Nish, since Nish was walking back-wards – was Lars Johansson. Lars, Dmitri, and Andy, and Jenny in net, had already won their first game with an 11–3 victory over a weak threesome from Seattle.

Nish backed in, sweeping his arm low in a deep bow as Lars followed, laughing.

"The Master of 3-on-3 will now address us!" Nish announced.

Lars blushed slightly and plunked himself down on a bench. "Muck asked me to talk to you," he said. "This is going to be different from any-thing you guys have ever done before. A couple of practices don't prepare you for how quick it's going to be and how confusing it can get."

"Your team had no trouble," said Sarah.

"We were up against three big kids who couldn't skate with us," Lars said. "Muck says your opponent is going to be one of the top teams."

Nish looked up, confused, moving his head quickly from side to side.

"Who *are* we up against?" he asked.

"The Portland Panthers," Sarah said. "Ring a bell, big boy?"

"No!" Nish shouted up from tying his skates. "Should it?"

"Lake Placid?" Sarah said.

"Billings and Yantha?" Travis said.

Nish looked up, blinking, and Travis could see it was all coming back to him: Billings, the shifty little defenceman on the team that had almost beaten the Owls at the Lake Placid tournament; Yantha, the big centre with the booming shot.

"Wedgies . . . ," Sarah said, encouraging Nish to remember. "The time you rewired the hotel television . . ."

Nish was already blushing. "Okay, okay, okay – I remember. Big deal. We beat them then, we'll beat them now."

"Not the same thing at all," Lars said.

"What makes *you* the big expert?" Nish challenged.

"He's played it more than any of us," Sarah said, defending Lars. But Lars's feelings weren't hurt. He was well used to Nish's big mouth.

"It's easy," Lars said. "For 3-on-3 you just have to remember three things."

"*Skate! Shoot! Score!*" Nish shouted.

No one paid him any attention. Lars counted off the three points on his fingers: "One, pass to open spaces. Two, use your body to create holes for your teammates. Three, don't be afraid to slow things down."

"*And four!*" Nish shouted. "*Fire the stupid puck in the stupid net!*"

Travis had never felt so big. He could see his reflection in the glass as he swept the length of the little rink in three hard, extended strides. If the Olympic-sized ice surfaces in Lake Placid and Sweden had seemed as big as a frozen lake, this was like a puddle.

He loved it. He and Sarah and Nish were swirling so fast during the warmup it felt dizzying. A shot on Jeremy, the next player in dropping the rebound for the next shot. Shot, rebound, drop, shot . . . He rang his third one off the crossbar: it was going to be a great game.

First, though, there was a small ceremony. The organizers came out onto the ice and a man said what Travis supposed were a few words of welcome into a microphone – the echo in the arena was so loud, Travis couldn't make out a word the man was saying – and then a man and woman came out pulling large boxes alongside them on the ice and handed out gifts to the players on both teams.

"T-shirts, I hope," said Nish.

"Looks like something much more than that," said Sarah.

She was right. It was far more, in fact, than Travis had ever heard of for a peewee tournament. He'd been given T-shirts before – they were Nish's favourite souvenir – and mugs and little trophies and even a set of kids' books about a hockey team that travels to tournaments all over and gets in all kinds of trouble. But he'd never been given anything like this.

First, each player was given a brand-new equipment bag, with the tournament logo and the player's number on either end.

"*Awesome!*" said Nish as he examined his treasured number, 44. "Just like the pros!"

And as if that weren't enough, there was also a second gift, in a black-and-gold presentation box.

Nish, of course, was into it like a small child at Christmas. He pulled out a round plastic ball that had water inside.

"Am I expected to drink this?" he shouted, exasperated.

Sarah, shaking her head, ripped it out of his hands, turned it over once, and handed it back.

Instantly the globe was filled with a swirling flurry of snow, the white flakes tumbling about in the liquid until they settled around a beautiful miniature scene of a ski hill.

"It's a souvenir of Grouse Mountain, dummy," she said. "Where they snowboard."

"*Ohhh*," said Nish, as if he'd never heard of such a thing. He turned the globe over, shook it hard, and watched the snow swirl and settle again. "*Outstanding!*" he said.

"Here," Mr. Dillinger said, holding out his hands. "Give me those bags. I'll be transferring the other kids' gear over to theirs, so I'll set yours up by your lockers so you can put all your stuff in after the game."

"What about our snow globes," asked Nish.

"Don't worry – I'll put them in the bags, too. For safe keeping."

Nish reluctantly handed over his equipment bag and new toy. Mr. Dillinger reboxed the globe and, with Lars's help, gathered up the other, unopened boxes and equipment bags from Jeremy and Sarah and Travis. The rest of the team could put their own away.

These four had a game to play.

6

TRAVIS PLACED HIS STICK ACROSS THE TOP OF HIS shin pads and coasted, looking down into the ice and off to the far end – which wasn't very far away – to check out the Panthers. He recognized Yantha immediately: big and dark and smooth. It looked as if he'd grown since Lake Placid. He looked at Billings, the quick little blond defence-man who was such a wonderful skater. Billings looked back, winked, and raised his stick in salute. He, too, had recognized his opponents. Travis remembered they'd exchanged autographs at the end of the Lake Placid tournament. He still had Billings's autograph. He wondered if Billings had kept his.

It felt funny. It felt weird. It felt neat. He was happy for the first time since they'd gone out whale watching and come upon the floating bodies. The two officials came out, and the little ice surface seemed magically filled with skaters. They lined up for the faceoff, Sarah to take it, Travis to the side, and Nish well back by Jeremy. It was, Travis thought, just like playing shinny in the basement.

But as soon as the referee dropped the puck, the novelty turned to challenge. With only three on the ice, the players were free to go anywhere, yet in such a small area, there were few hiding places, and no place to coast and suck up your wind. There were, as well, no changes, meaning they had to take a whole new approach to the game. You couldn't go flat out all the time. You had to pick your spots. You had to gather energy and not waste it. Never had Muck's warnings about "skating around in circles like chickens with their heads cut off" made more sense.

Muck was still coach, but it wasn't the same. With no changes, he could talk strategy only at the break. He could have yelled over the noise of the thin crowd, but Muck, of course, never yelled. Travis could hear Data screaming, and thought he heard Sam's big voice a couple of times, and once he heard Lars yelling for them to *slow it down!*

Lars's instructions were making more sense than they had in the dressing room. With the Owls swirling and the Panthers sticking with them, there was little point in direct passing. Better to drop it in an open space when you could see that Nish or Sarah was headed that way. Travis also found he was most effective in leaving passes and using his body to brush away his checker. But as for the advice to slow things down – how was that possible?

The games were two periods, twenty minutes of straight running time each, and at the break all six players and the two goaltenders simply collapsed onto their backs in exhaustion. They'd been going full out for most of the period, pausing only for the faceoffs and after goals. The two teams were almost perfectly balanced, with five goals for the Panthers, including a spectacular backhand roofer by Billings, and five for the Owls, including three pretty dekes by Sarah.

Travis's lungs were burning, but he felt wonderful. The game had been spectacular – fun and clean, quick and well-played, like both a championship game and a Sunday afternoon on the frozen creek at home. He felt the pressure to win, but it came from himself and his teammates, not from the stands. And there was none of that terror of making a mistake that so often turned regular hockey games into dull demonstrations of how to dump a puck in and how to chip it back out.

Muck said something during the break that Travis never expected to hear coming out of his coach's mouth: "You're too predictable."

Travis blinked, the salt of his sweat biting into his eyes. He was surprised at how much he was sweating.

"Try something they're not expecting," Muck said.

A hundred games of being coached by Muck flashed before Travis Lindsay's eyes. He remembered the back pass that Muck had so hated. He remembered Muck's frown when he tried that silly little dance of the puck off his skate blades. But now here was Muck telling Travis to cut loose. Use a little driveway ingenuity. Try some of those basement tricks.

The Panthers went ahead in the second, and final, period on two quick goals by Yantha, one of which almost ripped Jeremy's arm off before bouncing through and over the line. Nish scored on a pass that accidentally clipped off Billings's skate, and Sarah hit the goal post on a backhand after she'd cleanly beaten the Panthers' goaltender.

Travis tried everything. He lost the puck in his own skates trying to click it up onto his blade, and Billings picked it off and scored. He tried a back pass, but Yantha read it perfectly and used Nish for a screen, firing a puck between Nish's legs that found the far corner of the net.

The Panthers had a three-goal lead and Travis could hear the crowd getting louder. He could hear Data's anxious, high-pitched voice calling for them to get going. But no sound came from Muck. Even if the Owls were down by ten goals, Muck would never shout.

Sarah picked up a rebound that Jeremy fed to the corner, then flipped the puck back into the far corner for Nish. Without even looking, Nish dumped the puck cross ice and bounced it off the boards for Sarah in full flight. She flew down the wing and blew a slapshot past the Panthers' goaltender to reduce the lead to two.

With five minutes left and the tension rising, the Owls took their game up a level. Nish stick-handled end to end before slipping a drop pass back between his own legs to Travis, and Travis threw a quick pass across the crease to Sarah, who scored again.

A minute left, and Nish scored on a fabulous rush that forced Yantha to trip him as he flew past the Panthers' big centre. Nish managed to take the shot by sweeping his stick blindly across the ice, but a second later crashed heavily into the boards.

Travis hated that sound. No, it wasn't the sound at all; it was the *silence* he hated at the end of a bad fall. It was as if all the noises of the arena – the skating, the yelling, the crowd, the whistles, the puck on blades, the crash of the sliding body into the boards, the echoes – all suddenly came to a stop, with every breath in the building held for fear of losing all breath entirely.

Both Sarah and Travis raced for their fallen teammate. Muck was already over the boards and making his way across the ice, Mr. Dillinger, with the first-aid kit, slipping and sliding along behind him.

"Anyone in the crowd holding a video camera?" Nish asked as Travis and Sarah leaned over.

"*What?*" said Travis. He wondered how badly Nish had smashed his head into the boards.

"I wanna know if anyone caught my goal," Nish said.

Sarah shook her head. "You're *pathetic*."

Nish grinned up, sweat covering his face. "I know," he said with enormous pride.

Mr. Dillinger checked him over. The referee checked him over. They decided that nothing was broken and helped Nish to his feet. Sarah picked up his stick, Travis his gloves. The crowd began cheering, and the Panthers, led by Yantha, pounded their sticks on the ice in tribute.

Travis felt proud of his friend – right up until Nish began blowing kisses to the crowd like he was some famous actor taking a curtain call.

"Next time, I might hit him myself," Sarah said, shaking her head.

Nish skated about for nearly a minute, then lifted his stick towards the referee to signal he had his wind back and was ready to finish the game.

The puck dropped and Sarah clipped it right out of the air back to Nish, who turned and raced back towards his own end.

"*You're goin' the wrong way, idiot!*" Sam's big voice bellowed through the rink. Travis could hear them laughing in the stands.

But Nish knew exactly what he was doing. With Yantha giving chase and the Panthers' other forward trying to cut off his passing lane to Sarah, Nish used the net to shake free of Yantha and, reversing suddenly, headed to the far side, with Yantha now trying to cut back across ice to head him off.

It was a brilliant tactic. The other forward, thinking Yantha was out of position, moved to cut off Nish. Nish waited, teasing with the puck on the end of his stick, and just as both Panthers came down on him, he flipped a backhand saucer pass that hit Sarah perfectly as she moved through centre.

Sarah snapped a quick pass to Travis, who moved over the blueline with it, Billings trying to stay level between the two rushing Owls.

Travis faked a pass to Sarah, but Billings was too smart to bite. He wasn't playing the puck; he was playing the zone, trying to stay between the two so Travis couldn't slip a pass across the crease to Sarah and would have to take a shot from well out.

Travis pulled the puck back tight to his skates and cut for centre. Sarah, reading him perfectly, cut from the opposite direction, hoping the criss-cross might confuse Billings.

But again, Billings was too smart. He kept to his position, and just as the two Owls began to cross, he began to go down, hoping to use his falling body to block the drop pass he believed Travis was planning.

Travis held. He held, and everything seemed to slow. He held, and Sarah blew past him, and Billings, already committed, went down onto his side, spinning perfectly to cut off the pass that never came.

Travis held, and drifted. As he slowed, everything else sped up, and instantly he understood what Lars had meant. Going slow, as long as it surprises, can open up space just as surely as speed can.

He was all alone now. Sarah had cut across, her skates now rasping on a hard turn. Billings was lost, his stick teasing helplessly like the sword of a defeated warrior.

The goaltender's pads stuttered. Travis held still, and waited. He seemed to be drifting like an astronaut, defying gravity, and the goalie, rattled by this neverending pause, gambled by flopping to his side and stacking his pads.

In a normal game, with two defencemen pressing him in the slot, Travis would have panicked and shot, praying the puck would somehow trickle through.

But this was not a normal game. This was 3-on-3 hockey, with everyone else out of the play, just Travis and the Panthers' goaltender alone with a slow-moving puck and a waiting net.

He held, seemingly forever, and continued to drift: past the goaltender's stick, past the stacked pads, past the skate blades until, finally, there was a small unblocked channel into the net.

Travis fired a backhand, low along the ice.

He heard so many sounds at once it was almost impossible to separate one from another: the horn, a whistle, cheering, cursing, Sarah screaming as she cut behind the net from the other side.

"TRAAAAVISSSS!"

Travis spun, his back slamming hard into the boards, but he felt nothing. He could see the referee, his hand pointing to the back of the net. He could see Yantha roaring back up ice, slamming his stick angrily. He could see the dejected look of the Panthers' goaltender, beaten.

The Screech Owls number-one team had won its first game.

They shook hands as the Zamboni came out to clean the ice. Yantha just slapped at Travis's glove, but Billings took his hand warmly.

"Nice goal, Travis," he said.

"Thanks," Travis said. He couldn't believe the little Portland defenceman still knew his name. Perhaps he had kept the card with its autograph – but he hadn't the nerve to ask.

The other Owls came onto the ice in their street clothes: Muck, Mr. Dillinger, Sam pushing through like she owned the place, then Lars.

Travis and Lars high-fived at centre ice.

"Slow enough for you?" Travis asked.

"It worked, didn't it?" Lars laughed.

"Perfectly."

7

NEVER HAD TRAVIS SEEN A TOURNAMENT SO wonderfully run. The organizers even took each team's equipment after the players switched over to the new tournament bags, and special locked "cages" had been provided in a rear storage area so teams could, if they wished, keep their equipment at the main tournament rink. Sarah and Sam, for example, wanted to take their equipment back to the motel and wash things out in the laundry room. Nish, red-faced, said he wanted to do the same and yanked his new pride and joy – "Official Competitor, First International 3-on-3 Hockey Tournament, Vancouver, B.C., No. 44" – off the nearest trolley, threw it over his shoulder, and headed out to catch the bus back to the motel.

"Nish has never washed his stuff in his life," noted Data as several of the Owls watched, astounded.

"He always says his stink is his good luck," said a mystified Jesse.

"He just wants to play with his new toy," said Travis. He made shaking motions with his hands and pretended to turn over a snow globe, his eyes widening in mock amazement.

"Didn't he have a childhood?" Wilson asked.

"He's still having it," said Sarah. "It's his missing adulthood that worries me."

The motel was simple, but nice, with a good view of English Bay and, on the far side, the green edge of Stanley Park. Sarah and Sam headed down to the laundry facilities to wash their hockey gear, Data and a few of the players started up a Nintendo round-robin, and Lars and Travis, who were rooming with Nish and Andy, lay down for a quick nap before dinner.

Travis was just dozing off when the quiet was broken by a cursing, angry Nish.

"*Damn it, damn it, damn it!*" Nish wailed. He sounded truly upset.

"*What?*" Travis shouted.

"My snow globe's broken!"

Travis sat up. At the foot of his bed was Nish, crouching over his new equipment bag. The box his snow globe had come in was torn at his feet and the beautiful gift in his hands.

"What's wrong?" Travis asked.

"Look!" Nish said, holding it up.

Travis stared at the snow globe. Only the snow inside wasn't swirling. It wasn't tumbling or falling.

It was doing nothing. More a solid snowball than a snowfall.

"What happened?" asked Travis.

"I dunno," said Nish. "I just pulled it out and it was busted."

Lars was already on his feet. He took the globe from Nish and rolled it over slowly in his hands. Nothing moved. "You must have shaken it awfully hard," he said.

"I didn't shake it at all," Nish protested.

"Maybe it got shaken on the bus," suggested Travis. "Or when they threw it on that trolley."

"That's probably it," said Lars, nodding. "It got so badly shaken it crystallized."

"*What?*" Nish asked, his face twisting into a puzzled prune.

"Crystallized," repeated Lars. "Sometimes things that are in liquid can crystallize and turn solid. Kind of like ice – only it doesn't need the cold."

Nish looked baffled. But he seemed to accept Lars's explanation. "I guess," he said. "But I don't want a broken one. I want a good one."

Lars smiled. "You can have mine. I don't care about it. I just like the equipment bag."

Nish looked relieved. "You're sure?"

"Sure. I'll give you mine next time we're back at the rink. It's in my new bag. That's where the rest of us put them."

Nish took back the broken snow globe and stared at it. "What'll we do with this one?"

"Put it in the drawer," Lars said. "Maybe I'll show it to someone and try to get a replacement."

43

Nish nodded. Perhaps he didn't understand crystallization, but he understood what he needed to know: that he would have a good, working snow globe to take home to his mother. Travis grinned slightly to himself. He knew Nish too well. If only the others knew what a big softie Nish was when it came to his mom. It was good of Lars to make such a generous offer – but then, that was typical of Lars, too. Always helping out. Always doing the right thing.

There was a loud rap on the door.

"You in there, Travis?" a voice called.

It was Sarah.

"Yeah, whadya want?"

"Muck wants to see us all down in the lobby – right away."

8

THE REST OF THE OWLS WERE ALREADY HANGING around the lobby. A few parents were there as well – only a handful had made the long trip – and Mr. Dillinger was organizing coffee. Muck was deep in conversation with a heavy-set, grey-haired man in a dark blue suit. Waiting to one side, both with Styrofoam cups of coffee steaming in their hands, were two other, powerful-looking men, also in dark suits.

Muck moved to the centre of the floor and cleared his throat. Everyone fell silent at once; they all wanted to know what was up.

"This here," said Muck, again clearing his throat as he turned to the grey-haired man, "is Inspector Bronson of the Royal Canadian Mounted Police. He's going to fill you in on what's been happening regarding the . . . incident."

Inspector Bronson, ruddy-faced and smiling, rubbed his hands nervously as he took his place beside Muck. He introduced the two men who had come with him, also with the RCMP.

"This has been a complicated investigation," said the inspector. "We've tried to co-ordinate matters, but it's also involved the Coast Guard, City of Victoria Police, and the Department of Oceans and Fisheries. We've also been helped out by the good people at the Aquarium.

"I also want to thank you all for your valuable contribution. If you hadn't sighted that body —"

"Two bodies," a voice interrupted.

Travis turned sharply. It was Sam, her green eyes flashing with something very near anger.

The inspector's red face turned even redder.

"Yes, well, of course," he sputtered, the air before him raining with spittle. "But we're conducting a murder investigation, miss. For the purposes of that, we are speaking of one deceased . . . Mr. Bradley Cummings."

"The dolphin was murdered, too," protested Sarah.

"Yes, well," the inspector began. A fleck of white foam danced ridiculously on his bottom lip as he fumbled for his words. The girls had clearly thrown him off. "The dolphin was killed, we have now ascertained, by fishermen's nets. The animal pathologists at the Aquarium found rope burns on it. We believe that Mr. Cummings was engaged in some sort of effort to rescue the fish from the netting —"

"A dolphin's not a fish!" Sam insisted.

"Whatever, miss," the inspector smiled lamely. "Mr. Cummings was vitally involved in dolphin projects at the Aquarium and was known to go out often on his own in search of them.

"He was a card-carrying member of Greenpeace," the inspector added, with a hint of a sneer as he mentioned the well-known environmental protection group, "and had been involved in disputes with drift-net fishermen in the past. He was a key leader in the fight to have them banned."

"What happened?" asked Fahd.

"We don't know exactly what happened, son, but what we *believe* happened is that Mr. Cummings came upon a fishing boat illegally using drift nets. Perhaps he tried to challenge them in some way. Some of these Greenpeace guys can be quite aggressive, you know."

It was clear that the inspector had no use for Greenpeace. He spoke as if everyone in the room shared his opinion, though Travis doubted any did – with the possible exception of the two policemen standing by the doorway.

"We imagine there was a confrontation. We think it was settled with a gun."

"But why shoot the dolphin, too?" asked Sam.

The inspector turned, blinking with surprise. He shrugged. "Perhaps to put him out of his misery. We don't know exactly, of course. All we do know, and all we are investigating, miss, is that someone shot Mr. Cummings and killed him. Through the Coast Guard, we are now conducting a thorough search of the waters around the area in question. All fishing vessels will be searched."

"You expect to find the weapon?" Muck asked.

"If we do, we'll find the killer," the inspector said smugly.

"Wouldn't the gun be at the bottom of the ocean by now?" said Fahd.

"Not necessarily, son," the inspector said, glad to have sensible questions from a sensible young man like Fahd. "Some fishermen believe in the law of the high seas. They might feel perfectly entitled to defend their property with firearms."

"It's hardly like Brad was out to torpedo them!" Sam shot back.

The inspector turned, staring hard, his colour rising again. He clearly did not like to be interrupted, especially with sarcasm.

"Where is his boat?" Sarah asked.

"Whose boat?" the inspector snapped.

"Brad's."

"We have found no vessel," he said.

"Isn't that a bit odd?" Sarah asked.

There was spittle again on the inspector's lips, dancing as he blew out impatiently.

"It's a very big ocean, my dear," he said, as if speaking to a little child. "Things can get lost at sea. They can even sink. Perhaps they sank his boat after they shot him."

"But *why* shoot the dolphin!" Sam demanded, all but stomping her feet.

9

TRAVIS BLINKED SEVERAL TIMES, UNABLE TO believe his eyes. Maybe he'd lost his mind and was seeing things. Perhaps he was having a nightmare.

"What's wrong with *you*?" a familiar voice whined.

But there was nothing wrong with Travis. It was the *thing* standing in front of him that had a problem.

Whatever it was, it was standing in the harsh light of the motel room's bathroom door. It was wearing a floppy bucket cap with the Vancouver Canucks logo in the middle. It had mirror sunglasses on, sending Travis a reflection of himself, his mouth and eyes wide open in shock. It was wearing a thick smear of white sunscreen right down its nose and onto one cheek. It was carrying a small gym bag – again, Vancouver Canucks colours, Vancouver Canucks logo – and out of the top of the gym bag stuck a huge bottle of blue Gatorade, an opened plastic bag of long red licorice sticks, and the earphones to a portable CD player.

Over its shoulder it wore a gaudy orange-and-yellow towel – *and apart from that nothing else!*

Not a stitch.

"*What're you looking at?*" the familiar voice whined from behind the sunscreen and mirror sunglasses.

Travis wasn't exactly sure. The big mirror on the bathroom door played off the wall of mirrors over the sink, so that Travis was staring at not just one shocking, incredible sight, but at more than two dozen. *More than two dozen buck-naked Wayne Nishikawas!*

Nish smiled. "You coming with me?"

"Coming *with* you?" Travis said incredulously. "*Where?*"

"Wreck Beach, stupid."

"*Where?*"

"The nude beach. I checked at the front desk. It's just past the university – about a dozen blocks from here."

"You're not going like *that*?"

"What's wrong with this?" Nish asked, twirling like a fashion model. "I'm dressed perfectly for Wreck Beach. Sun's shining – perfect beach weather."

"How you gonna get there?"

Nish turned and looked at himself in the mirror – hat, sunglasses, towel, sandals, *nothing* else . . .

"You plan to *walk*?" Travis asked, laughing. He could just picture Nish waddling down the street, bare cheeks wobbling behind him, cars honking and swerving, police sirens screaming.

Nish shook his head with pity for Travis. "I'm not that dumb, you know. This is how I'll look when I get there. What do you think?"

"I think you're crazy. They'll never let you on – you're a kid!"

"And kids can't be nudists? Is that what you're saying?"

"Nobody's going to be there. It's still spring, for heaven's sake!"

"It's warm out. Nobody's going to freeze their pinkies off."

Travis rolled his eyes. "It's not your pinkie I'm thinking of."

Nish wasn't even listening. He was looping a big unbuttoned shirt over his shoulders and kicking around his dumped luggage for his bathing suit. He was getting dressed to go out – getting dressed to go out and get undressed.

"Are you coming?" he asked as he lifted the bathing suit on one sandalled toe.

"Not a chance, pal."

Nish stepped into the suit, shrugging. "Suit yourself – but it's the chance of a lifetime."

"To see *you* naked? I've already seen enough of that to last a lifetime!"

Travis had no idea what would become of Nish. Nor did he much care. Some of the other Owls were gathering in the lobby, getting ready to strike out for the nearest McDonald's and talking excitedly about the 3-on-3 tournament.

There was a buzz to this competition that Travis had never before experienced. At every other tournament, the Owls had talked about their own team, and other teams, and how they were doing, and who they might meet if they made it to the finals. But now that they were split into teams within teams, all the talk was about themselves. Gordie, Fahd, and Sam had two easy wins in the Canucks Division, and Derek, Liz, and Willie had won one and then been beaten badly in the Rockies Division.

Dmitri, Andy, and Lars were soon to play their third match in the Elite Division, after losing their second. This one would be against the Portland Panthers, who had already been beaten by Travis, Sarah, and Nish. Travis's team was now 2–0, as was Jesse's team, with Simon and Wilson.

The Owls' excited chatter was brought to an abrupt end by a loud rumble of thunder. Travis looked out and saw that dark clouds were moving in fast. It amazed him how quickly the weather could change in Vancouver. A few minutes ago there had been bright sunshine – "beach weather," Nish had called it – and now it looked like it was going to storm. What was it the motel manager had said to them the other day? "You don't like our weather? Wait five minutes and it'll change – I guarantee it."

They decided they'd better head for McDonald's before the rain hit, and were just on their way out when Sarah and Sam burst in, their arms filled with newspapers. They seemed very excited. Sarah was holding out the front page of the *Vancouver Sun*, tapping her finger hard against the headline.

"AQUARIUM SCIENTIST HAILED AS HERO."

"*They're saying Brad gave his life for the dolphin!*" she shouted.

Sam handed out copies with the front-page stories and photographs of Brad Cummings. There were quotes from his fellow workers, who all said Brad went out on the water every chance he got, searching for dolphins and warning fishing trawlers to stay away from spots where he'd seen them swimming.

There was talk of naming a park after Brad, talk of a special scholarship fund being set up at the university to encourage the study of endangered species. Travis read all the reports, and while he still felt terrible about what had happened to Brad – could barely stand to think of him rolling about in those waves with that hideous black hole in his chest – he felt proud of what Brad had been doing and happy that there were people who had appreciated his efforts. He was, indeed, a hero.

Sam was in tears reading one of the papers. It was a story about Brad's mother and how Brad had always cared for her and how, ever since he was a little boy, he had cared more for wild creatures than for anything else. There was even a picture of a young Brad, aged thirteen or fourteen, feeding one of the killer whales at the Aquarium, and Sam clutched the newspaper picture to her heart as if she were about to faint.

"Listen to this!" shouted Data, who had wheeled over and picked up a copy of the *Vancouver Province*.

Just then there was a tremendous clap of thunder and a roar as the rain burst outside. Travis was glad Sarah and Sam had come along with the papers. They'd saved them from a soaking.

"'COAST GUARD FOLLOWING LEAD IN CUM-MINGS MURDER,'" Data read, almost having to shout over the rain drumming on the motel windows. "'The Canadian Coast Guard has stopped and searched more than twenty fishing boats and trawlers in the past two days in an effort to find more details on the death of Bradley Cummings, twenty-seven, the marine biologist who was found floating off Victoria Harbour Monday with a bullet hole in his chest.

"'The RCMP Forensic Division in Vancouver has tentatively identified the murder weapon as an old-fashioned .303 Lee Enfield rifle, a war weapon once popular with deer hunters.

"'According to sources, the Coast Guard has interviewed at least two witnesses who reported hearing a shot, or several shots, fired in the vicinity Monday morning. Numerous fishing vessels – Canadian, American, Japanese, and Russian – were reportedly fishing in adjacent waters at the time.

"'Officials hope to find the weapon involved. A rifle, however, is easily lost to deep waters, and the Coast Guard is aiming its investigation more at interviews and possible eye-witnesses.'"

"Let's hope they find the murderer," said Wilson.

"I still can't understand why they'd shoot the dolphin, too," said Sam.

"You care more about a fish than a person?" asked Simon.

"It's not a fish. It's a dolphin. And of course I care about Brad – I just don't understand why they'd do that to a dolphin."

"It was caught in their nets," suggested Data, "and that's how they get rid of them. It was going to die anyway. Brad must have heard the shot and come after them. Or maybe he saw them do it. And then they shot him."

"I hope they catch them," said Liz.

"So do I," said Sarah.

"*What the hell is that?*" howled Derek, staring in the direction of the glass front door.

The Screech Owls all turned at once. The door opened, wind and rain bursting in as if someone had turned a fire hose on the motel entrance.

And with the wind and rain came a strange wet creature. It put its back to the door, pushing hard to close it. The latch caught, shutting the storm outside, and the room filled with silence. Silence but for the huffing and puffing of the creature who had burst in.

It wore a soaked bucket hat that hung so limp over the creature's face they couldn't see its eyes. There was something white smeared down its nose and cheeks. There was an unbuttoned shirt, wet through and clinging like paint to the heaving chest of whatever was beneath it. There was a bathing suit, halfway down the creature's hips, heavy with water and threatening to drop. There was a dripping sports bag, a half-finished bottle of blue Gatorade sticking out past the dangling earphones of a portable CD.

"*Nish?*" Sam ventured.

Travis said nothing. He didn't need the creature to speak to know what it was.

The creature was shaking and shivering right in front of them. Its teeth were clicking together. It was moaning.

"*Where were you?*" Sarah asked.

The soaking wet bucket cap came off, revealing a very wet Wayne Nishikawa. He wiped the back of his arm across his face, smearing the white sunscreen from ear to ear.

"Nowhere," he mumbled through chattering teeth.

"*You weren't looking for that nude beach, were you, Nish?*" Sam demanded loudly.

Everyone started laughing.

"*None of your business!*" Nish practically spat.

"Whadya see, Nish," Andy teased, "bare-naked . . . *ducks?*"

Nish scowled in Andy's direction. He shook himself like a big dog and started to walk towards the corridor leading to his room. His sandals squished as he stepped, large, wet footprints mapping his progress.

Nish paused at the doorway, peeled off his drenched shirt and shook it, spraying water in the Owls' direction without so much as turning around.

His wet bathing suit had slipped down even further, his cheeks bulging above the elastic. He stuck his bum out, half-mooning the Owls.

"I'M GONNA HURL!" howled Sam.

10

TRAVIS'S TEAM WAS SCHEDULED TO PLAY ITS
third game in the Elite Division, this time against
a spunky little side from Boston that had already
beaten one of the better Canadian teams in the
tournament. Muck and Data had "scouted" the
Boston threesome in its previous game, and
Muck asked the Owls' top team, plus Jeremy, to
show up early to go over a few points with him.

Nish and Sarah carried their new equipment
bags over their shoulders. Sarah had washed her
jersey and socks and aired her equipment, and
Travis could smell Fleecy fabric conditioner
wafting up from her bag. Travis couldn't think of
many peewee players who actually washed their
gear. He might "air out" his stuff once or twice,
but most of the players here, he figured, wouldn't
even think to check their equipment from the
day they arrived to the day they left. Still, it was
such a pleasant change from Nish's equipment,
which usually smelled like a giant's armpit
whenever he unzipped it in the change room
and dumped the damp, unwashed contents out

in a huge pile. Nish, of course, had done nothing to his equipment, despite his threats. He'd only wanted to get his hands on the snow globe, which had also proved to be a huge disappointment.

They took over a small dressing room at the far end of the corridor. Mr. Dillinger helped Travis collect his new equipment bag – with the number 7 sharp on both ends – from the locked storage section that had been assigned to the Owls, and when he came back to the room Nish was staring down at his freshly dumped equipment in total shock.

No smell whatsoever.

No stink, no crumpled, caked socks, no damp, sticking sweater, no rolls of shin-pad tape, no half-empty bottles of Gatorade, no candy-bar wrappers – nothing to identify this as the pride and joy of Wayne Nishikawa, number 44, Screech Owls.

"What the hell's going on here?" Nish demanded.

"I can't believe it," said Jeremy. "Your equipment bag's open and I'm not gagging."

"*It's not my equipment!*" Nish whined.

"You're number 44," Travis said, gently kicking the end of the bag where Nish's number was clearly stitched.

"But look at the stuff!" Nish protested. "It's all brand new!"

Nish was right. New shin pads, new shoulder pads, new pants, new skates, new socks, new helmet, new gloves, new rolls of tape, garters, jock, everything.

"It's never been used," said Jeremy.

"That's crazy!" said Nish. "That makes no sense."

"Wait a minute!" Travis interrupted. He had just thought of something. "Where'd you get the bag from?"

"They *gave* them to us, remember?"

"No, no, no – I mean, where'd you get it from when you picked it up to go back to the motel?"

Nish looked puzzled. "Off the cart. Mr. Dillinger was just about to put them away, remember?"

"Yeah, I do. But the Panthers were putting theirs away at the same time. You're positive you got yours off the right cart?"

"Yeah – I guess," Nish said, but he didn't sound very sure.

"Mr. Dillinger's still out there," Jeremy said. "He's setting up his skate sharpener."

"He'll know," suggested Travis. "Let's go check with him."

They went into the corridor and down to the storage area, where Mr. Dillinger was already at work on a skate, a long spray of red-orange sparks shooting out from the blade as he expertly drew it along the spinning stone. Data was with him, lining up the skates as Mr. Dillinger finished sharpening them.

Mr. Dillinger shut the sharpening machine off when he saw them and lifted his safety glasses, smiling.

"We think Nish got the wrong bag," Travis said.

Mr. Dillinger chuckled. "Pretty hard to mistake Nish's equipment for anyone else's, isn't it?"

"Very funny," Nish said. "I took it off the cart – but this is what I ended up with."

He tossed the equipment bag down in front of Mr. Dillinger, the brand-new shin pads sticking up through the opened zipper. Mr. Dillinger leaned over and drew a deep, contented breath, like a man taking the first smell of spring.

"It isn't Nish's stuff – that I assure you," Mr. Dillinger said.

"Where'd my stuff go?" Nish asked.

"Maybe it's still on our cart," suggested Jeremy.

"That's where I got *this* one," Nish argued.

"Maybe you took it from the Panthers' cart. Don't forget – they got new bags at the same time."

Mr. Dillinger considered a moment. "It's possible," he said. "Why don't I just check our stuff to make sure."

He laid down the skate he'd been holding and fumbled in his pockets for a key chain. He picked out a shiny new key and headed back down to the storage locker. The others, including Data, followed.

He worked the key quickly into the lock, opened up the gate, and entered. The three players followed him in. Mr. Dillinger pushed and pulled at various bags. He reached deep in the pile and tugged hard at one buried near the bottom. With a grunt he pulled it free.

"There she be," said Mr. Dillinger, moving aside so they could see a large white number 44 on one end.

"Let me check," said Nish, pushing his way through.

He reached over and unzipped the bag. He breathed deep, imitating Mr. Dillinger, the smell like fresh-baked bread to him. "I'm home!" Nish announced.

"Zip it up!" Mr. Dillinger said. "You're peeling the paint off the walls!"

Nish snorted and zipped his bag up. He threw it over his shoulder and bounced the weight happily. He had his equipment back.

"Leave the other one with me," said Mr. Dillinger. "I'll be seeing the Panthers' manager – they play right after you. I just hope they didn't need it before this."

"It's just extra equipment," said Nish. "Brand new stuff just in case, I guess. They wouldn't have needed it."

"Lucky for you, young man," said Mr. Dillinger. "Lucky for you."

Nish was happily getting into his wretched equipment when Muck and Data arrived with Sarah. They all pushed into the little dressing room and Muck went over some last-minute reminders for the three players and their goalie.

"They've got one great shooter," said Muck, "and they won their first match by setting him up in the slot. There's a young woman on the team who's quick but doesn't see the ice nearly as well as you, Sarah. And their third is the most incredible pest you're every going to see on the ice. He never stops working, and he's going to get to you, Mr. Nishikawa, unless you promise to put a lid on that temper of yours."

Nish blinked and smiled like a choirboy. "You can't be talking about me, coach, surely . . ."

Muck shook his head. "Their goalie's good, but I think he's weak on low shots."

"I *know* he's weak on low shots," said Data. He was consulting a detailed scouting report spread across his knees. If hockey could be reduced to a mathematical equation, thought Travis, Data would be the one to calculate it. Unfortunately, there were two elements of the game that could never be figured out entirely, never reduced to simple equations: surprise and luck. Though without those two unknowns, figured Travis, hockey wouldn't be near the delight it is, both to those who play and to those who are just fans.

"He had eight scored on him last game," said Data. "Of the twelve shots on goal, seven were low – five right along the ice. He has the best glove hand I've ever seen – sorry, Jeremy."

"That's okay," Jeremy said, flapping his catching glove like a lobster claw.

Muck was ready to sum up: "Keep the big guy out of the slot. Watch the playmaker and try to surprise her. Don't let the checker pester you. And keep the shots low. Okay?"

"*Okay!*" they all said at once.

"Then let's go."

Muck and Data had done their job. From the moment the puck dropped it was clear that the Boston team was like a one-song band: let the shooter find the slot, feed him the puck, and let him shoot. Not very imaginative, Lars would have said, but it had worked before and, despite Muck's and Data's warnings, was working again against the Owls' top threesome.

Boston was up 3–0 before the Owls even managed a good shot on goal. In part it was Jeremy's fault – maybe Data had put him off by saying how good the other goalie was – but it was also Travis's fault for letting the playmaker get away from him, Sarah's fault for letting the slot stay open, and Nish's fault for letting the chippy little checker get to him. Nish had already swung his stick hard at the little checker's heels.

"You connect with one of those swings and you could be kicked out of the game," said Muck. "You might want to consider that, young man."

Nish never lost it again. He began to play as only Nish could play, when he wanted to. He was cool, methodical, careful, smart. He blocked shot after shot from the shooter. He fooled the playmaker by letting her think she had room to pass, only to dive and frustrate her best efforts. He ignored the chippy checker, who soon seemed much closer to losing his temper than Nish was.

Sarah scored on a high backhander. Travis scored on a shot that never left the ice, causing a loud "*Whoop!*" from Data. And Nish scored on an end-to-end rush where he pulled the goalie out and gently tucked the puck in behind him as if he were placing an egg back in the refrigerator.

"Now we've got a game," Muck said. He was almost smiling.

It was a game indeed. Travis kept tight to the playmaker, making sure she had little ice to work with, and tried to force her to dump the puck to empty space. Sarah, with her great speed, was able to beat the others to loose pucks, which she then got to Nish, letting him work as a kind of quarterback as they moved up the ice.

Travis tried to keep in mind what Lars had told them. He used location passes. He used his body well. And he used slowness as a tactic, which worked beautifully.

It was on Travis's second goal that he realized the goaltender was guessing where the shot would go. The goalie had got it right almost every time, until Travis discovered the slightest pause could cause him to drop down, stack his pads, and even drift right out of the net.

"*Keep it! Keep it! Keep it!*" Travis whispered to Nish and Sarah as they lined up for the faceoff. Both understood. Both began keeping more.

The Owls went ahead 5–3. Boston tied it up. The Owls went ahead on a lovely little deke from Travis. The Owls went two up on a rocket from Sarah that never left the ice. And the Owls went ahead to stay on a blistering slapshot from Nish that bounced off the checker *and* Travis before tumbling up over the fallen goalie and into the net.

Final score: Owls 9, Boston 6.

Sarah, Travis, and Nish – and Jeremy – were undefeated.

"Good work," Muck said when he and Data came into the dressing room. He was carrying cold cans of Coke, and handed them out. For Muck to do something like this, Travis figured, was roughly the equivalent of buying them all new cars and handing out Stanley Cup rings. He must have been delighted. He even opened Nish's drink for him, Nish pretending to be unconscious as he lay flat on his back with his feet up on the bench.

"I-have-got-to-let-the-blood-flow-back-to-my-head," he groaned.

"We'll let you know if it ever gets there," said Sarah.

Nish stuck his tongue out at her and guzzled from his Coke, the dark liquid running down his cheeks and onto the floor. He then burped, loud as a car backfiring – a sure sign he was happy with his game.

Mr. Dillinger came in and congratulated them all.

"Did you get the bag back?" asked Travis.

Mr. Dillinger scratched his head. "I tried," Mr. Dillinger said. "But it wasn't the Panthers' – they don't even have a number 44 on their team."

"Whose was it, then?" Nish asked from the floor.

"I don't know," said Mr. Dillinger. "And they don't know. I guess it was just an extra."

"That doesn't make any sense," said Data.

"I know it doesn't, son," said Mr. Dillinger. "But you explain it, then."

Data shrugged. He said nothing.

But Travis could tell from the look in Data's face that he wasn't going to be satisfied with no answer at all – not when there had to be an explanation for such a simple mistake.

11

TRAVIS DECIDED THIS TIME TO TAKE HIS equipment back to the motel. He was sure he had been sweating much more playing 3-on-3 hockey than he normally did. Not only was it a lot more fun and relaxed than regular games, it was harder work. There were no changes, no long breaks, fewer faceoffs – and only two other players on the ice to pick up the slack if you missed your check or dogged it backchecking. At the end of each game, Travis felt drained, and by the weight and smell of his equipment, he knew exactly where he had drained to: it was time to air out the equipment.

He obviously wasn't the only player with this in mind. A couple of the Boston players had their equipment slung over their backs. And Sarah was again taking hers with her. Not Nish, though. His recovered equipment was zipped up and festering at the back of the Owls' storage area.

"Hang on there a minute, son!"

Travis turned, not recognizing the voice.

A man was walking towards him fast. He had

on a dark bulky windbreaker and tinted glasses, the kind that seem to darken as the wearer moves from shadow to light, from inside to outside. He had a buzz-cut, his hair clipped so close his scalp seemed to shine in the arena lights. He had one large earring in his left ear.

Nish was pushing through the door already and turned back as the man reached them.

The man was smiling. They could see a crest on the windbreaker now, a tournament crest. He was one of the organizers.

He held his hands out helplessly, almost signalling an apology. "Look, you'll have to excuse me," he said, "but I've been asked to do a quick check of every bag leaving the building. Would you mind, son, if I took just the quickest peek?"

"What's the problem?" Nish asked.

The man shrugged, smiling. "There's been a thief at work here the last few days. Couple of wallets. Some skates. Look, I'm not even suggesting it might be either of you guys – in fact, we think it's just someone creating mischief. You know, putting stuff in other guys' bags to get them in trouble. I can guarantee you no trouble – just a quick glance to be sure, okay?"

"Sure," said Travis. "Go ahead."

Travis slipped the bag off his shoulder and dropped it onto the smooth concrete floor of the entranceway.

"Thanks," the man said. He unzipped the bag, ran a hand quickly down both sides, checked the end pocket.

He pointed to Travis's tournament present, the boxed snow globe.

"That what they gave you?"

"Yeah," Travis answered.

"What're they like?" the man asked.

"Neat," said Travis. "It's a snow globe."

The man was already opening the box. He peered down at the snow globe, gave it a little shake, and laughed.

"I love these things," the man said.

Travis grinned. For an "official," this guy wasn't doing much of a job of checking things over. He seemed too easily distracted. He put the snow globe back in its box, carefully closed it, and returned it to Travis's bag.

"Thanks a lot," the man said. "Sorry to be such a hassle."

"No problem," Travis said.

He hoisted his bag up over his shoulder again, and Nish pushed open the doors and held them for Travis. It had been raining when they arrived, but now the sun was shining.

Nish was already babbling about getting back to Wreck Beach. He said he knew he'd never talk Travis into going with him, but perhaps Lars would go. Lars, after all, came from Sweden and was used to saunas and didn't think there was anything particularly odd or funny about walking around naked and . . .

But Travis wasn't even listening. Nish went on and on, and Travis tried to concentrate the way he would on a difficult math problem. This tournament was wonderful – in a way, he'd never enjoyed the game of hockey more – but there were also some very strange things going on around them.

The Owls had stumbled across a murder. Two murders, if you counted the dolphin. They knew the victim, even if only slightly. That was the first mystery, and now there was this second, completely different one.

Hockey bags.

Nish had walked off with a bag that didn't belong to him – and, as far as they could tell, didn't belong to *anyone*. And now this tough-looking man had asked to search through Travis's hockey bag with some weird story about stolen equipment. It hadn't rung true when he said it, and it didn't ring true now that Travis thought it over.

No, this was much worse than any math problem. In this case, nothing at all added up.

Lars met them in the motel lobby, holding out a snow globe with a perfect little blizzard inside. Nish grabbed it and kissed it. Now he had a present for his mother, and this one worked.

"Did you exchange it?" Nish asked.

"Nah – I'll ask about it later. You can have mine. I picked it up at the rink for you."

"They didn't accuse you of stealing it, did they?" asked Travis.

"No. Why do you say that?"

"They checked my bag on the way out."

"Mine, too," added Sarah.

"There was a guy at the door asked if he could see it," said Lars. "But he never said a word about stealing."

"Did he check it?" asked Travis.

"Yeah," Lars said, his voice trailing with wonder. "He said he just wanted to see how it worked."

"Same with me," said Sarah.

"Maybe there've been complaints about other globes that don't work," suggested Nish.

"Maybe," said Travis, but he didn't think so. Surely the man with the earring would have said something about faulty snow globes when he was looking at his. But instead, he'd acted as if he'd never seen one before, even though Travis was sure Sarah had left before Travis and Nish.

"This guy shaved practically bald, with a big earring?" Travis asked Sarah.

"Yeah," said Sarah. "Why?"

"I don't know – just wondering."

12

NISH WAS STILL GAZING AT HIS PERFECT NEW snow globe when the doors to the motel burst open and Sam roared in, brandishing the morning newspaper.

"*There's something weird going on here!*" she announced. She seemed both angry and determined at the same time.

"What is it?" Sarah asked.

"Just look at this!" Sam said. She spread the newspaper out on the lobby coffee table and her teammates clustered around, peering down at the place on the front page where she was tapping her finger.

"TIME OF DEATH A PUZZLE," said the headline. Sam read out loud:

"Medical experts have concluded that Brad Cummings, the twenty-seven-year-old marine biologist found murdered off Victoria Bay last weekend, died as much as three hours before the dolphin found shot in the same waters. Early investigation had been based on the assumption that the dolphin had been killed first.

"It had previously been presumed Mr. Cummings got into an argument over the fate of the dolphin, which led to a confrontation between the marine biologist, a known environmental activist, and fishermen who may have snagged the dolphin in illegal nets.

"The dolphin, Vancouver Aquarium scientists confirmed today, showed faint signs of abrasion on one side, consistent with injuries found among fish and animals that have struggled in fishing nets.

"Both victims, RCMP sources say, were killed with the same weapon, a Lee Enfield .303-calibre rifle once popular with local hunters.

"No weapon has been found, nor have any witnesses stepped forward in the case."

Sam finished reading and stood nodding with great satisfaction. "I knew there was something fishy about this whole thing," she said.

"Of course there was," Nish shot back. "They murdered a fish, remember?"

"You're too stupid to bother with," Sam said, dismissing him.

"I don't understand," said Fahd.

"Why would they kill Brad first?" Sam said. "It makes sense if he'd come along right *after* they'd shot the dolphin. Maybe he was even filming it. But why kill him and then, hours later, kill the dolphin?"

Everyone thought about it a while. No one had any idea why.

"Maybe they thought the dolphin knew something?" suggested Andy.

"Or *had* something?" offered Lars.

Sam looked up from the paper. "What do you mean?"

"I don't know," said Lars. "It just seems they must have had to chase the dolphin. Maybe it had run off with the nets?"

"I doubt that," said Andy.

"Well, something," said Lars.

"What?" Nish demanded.

"I don't know," said Lars. "Something."

It doesn't add up, Travis kept saying to himself. It just doesn't add up.

13

"LET'S GET NAKED!"

Nish was at the open window, ducking low to stare up into a soft blue sky. The sun had been out all morning, and the air pouring in was warm and filled with the promise of summer.

Nish was in his boxer shorts, visible to anyone in the parking lot who happened to pass by.

"Let's just get to the rink," Travis said. "You do what you want later – by yourself!"

"I think you should go see a psychiatrist," said Lars, flossing his teeth as he walked out of the bathroom.

"You can talk!" Nish barked back. "Only a nut would floss when there's no one to make him. I don't even brush my teeth when I'm on the road!"

"*Or shower!*" shouted Andy, who was just coming in from the hallway.

"*Or use deodorant!*" called out Wilson, right behind Andy.

Nish drew himself up and puffed out his chest. "That's because I believe in the cleansing power of nature. You see, *I* am a nudist!"

"You're a nudist *and* a nut," said Travis, surprising himself by saying so. "Now let's get dressed and get out of here. We want to see Gordie's group up against that team from California, don't we?"

"I'd rather see Wreck Beach!" protested Nish.

"You're pathetic!" said Andy.

The Owls had almost reached the little 3-on-3 rink when Travis, slightly ahead of the rest and helping push Data along, saw the quick flash of a Screech Owls sweater as someone ducked around the far corner of the arena, where the Zamboni came out to dump the snow.

"They're out back," Travis announced, turning and walking backwards as he informed the others.

With Travis and Data leading the way, the group headed down the side of the arena and around the corner to the rear of the building. Travis expected to find all four of the Owls who would playing that afternoon – Fahd, Andy, Sam, and, in goal, Jenny – but when he turned the corner he realized there was only the one.

Sam . . . smoking.

She turned when she heard them and coughed out a lungful of cigarette smoke. Travis could see she was trying to hide the burning cigarette behind her back, but then, realizing it was only the boys, she slyly drew her hand forward and attempted to look natural.

But it didn't look natural at all. It looked ridiculous. Especially with her dressed for a game of hockey.

"You'll stunt your growth," Data said.

"Mind your own business," said Sam.

Travis winced. He hadn't expected such a sharp response to Data's comment. He watched her face as she dragged deep on the cigarette. Her eyes were red; she looked like she might be on the verge of tears.

Was it the smoke? Or the murders? None of the Screech Owls had seemed as caught up in and upset about the murders as Sam had. Each morning she was up at dawn to grab the early papers. She listened to the newscasts. She had even phoned the Aquarium to see if there was any more information on the death of the dolphin. Twice she had exploded at teammates for talking about the "murder," as if the word could only apply to people. She referred to the "murders," and she grieved as much for the poor dolphin as she did for Brad Cummings.

Sam flicked the still-burning cigarette away. She coughed once but then held the smoke for some time before expelling it in a long, elegant plume that rose over her head and vanished into the air.

"Muck catches you, you're dead meat," said Nish.

"Muck catches me, I'll know who told," she said, and stomped in through the Zamboni doors towards the dressing room.

"What's with her?" Nish asked.

"She's upset," said Andy. "She's been like that ever since the whale watching."

"What can we do about it?" said Wilson. "The police are working on it."

"They're not getting anywhere," said Andy. "I think that's what's wrong with Sam. No one seems to care about the dolphin, and no one seems to be getting anywhere on the murder."

"Murders," corrected Data.

"Murders," agreed Andy.

"We better get inside," said Travis. He started to turn Data's chair around, but Data held up his hand for Travis to stop.

"Just leave me here," Data said. "I can get in the Zamboni entrance easier than the front."

"You're sure?" asked Travis.

"I'm sure. I want to check out something anyway."

Travis shrugged. He knew better than to hound Data about what he was up to. If Data wanted him to know, he would have said.

"Suit yourself," Travis said. "You know where we'll be."

14

DATA WAS HAPPY TO BE LEFT ALONE, TO MOVE at his own pace on Nish's great puzzle, which Data found both confusing and fascinating. Too many voices tended to cloud the issue, too many ideas sent his own mind in wild circles – but always, always returning to the one point that made no sense to him: the hockey bag that had no owner.

He kept his brain locked on that one troublesome fact. He wouldn't let his thoughts drift off to puzzling over why, or how, the man in the water might have died before the dolphin. He refused to think about the snow globes and why the organizers would have a man checking the players as they left the rink. These were significant factors – they might even turn out to be critical clues – but Data had a gut feeling he couldn't shake about the mysterious hockey bag.

Everything else might have an explanation. The man and dolphin might have been murdered by different people. The autopsy reports might even be wrong. And there might have been a problem with kids stealing from the tournament, even if Data had trouble believing they would do such a thing.

But there could be no easy explanation for the hockey bag. It wasn't Nish's, even though it was exactly the same as the one he'd been given and had his number on it. A mix-up would have been understandable, and at first that's what it had appeared to be. But once it turned out that the Panthers had no number 44, and the only trolley Nish could have gotten mixed up over was the Panthers' – all the other teams' equipment being locked up – it seemed to Data to make absolutely no sense at all.

But he had a notepad and he had a hunch. He rolled his wheelchair down past the dripping Zamboni, over a hose line, and down a corridor towards the large storage area at the back of the rink.

He could hear the high, dry song of a skate-sharpening machine. It didn't sound like Mr. Dillinger's, and he hoped it wasn't. He was looking for another equipment manager, from another team altogether.

He rolled as fast as he could towards the sound.

Travis, Nish, and the rest sat in the stands, cheering on their teammates – Fahd, Gordie, and Sam – against a tough, quick team from California, the Arrowhead Rangers.

"Fahd may finally have found his game," said Lars.

Travis nodded in agreement. It was somewhat surprising to see, but Lars was correct: in 3-on-3, Fahd was two or three times the player he was in regular hockey. Fahd had always moved so slowly and deliberately on the ice, but here, with more space to work in, his slowness worked at times to his advantage. It was just as Lars had said. And Fahd seemed able to keep track of his opponents far better when there were just three of them instead of five. He suddenly seemed smarter, niftier, slicker, and if he still lacked speed it was hardly a disaster, because, unlike in other games, he was always moving the puck just before an opposition player caught him.

Gordie and Sam were playing as expected. Gordie's long reach was a great advantage on the smaller rink, and he was able to read his team-mates well. And Sam, by sheer desire, was able to drive directly for the net from almost anywhere, panicking the Rangers so much they put two checkers on her, which only opened up either Fahd or Gordie for an easy pass and shot. And if the puck found Gordie, with his hard, quick wrist shot, it seemed to end up in the net every time.

The Owls' threesome, with Jenny in net, was up 5–2 at the break. Mr. Dillinger had come around and was sitting with the others, and he started up a great cheer for the skaters before the puck dropped again.

"Muck's betting they make the finals," said Mr. Dillinger when he sat back down beside Travis.

Travis looked to make sure Mr. Dillinger wasn't joking. He wasn't. He wasn't even looking to see Travis's reaction – if he had, he would have seen Travis's jaw drop.

The finals? Travis thought he had a pretty good fix on which threesomes were moving ahead, and he'd already figured on his own group, with Sarah and Nish; the Panthers' top threesome; the Owls' other elite team, Dmitri, Andy, and Lars; and perhaps a team from Winnipeg battling it out to see which two met in the "A" championship. He'd never for a moment considered one of the teams from the Canucks Division jumping up, even though they'd been told from the start that crossovers were possible. He'd figured the Elite Division had been given its name for a reason.

And yet he had to admit, they were playing extremely well. It was as if he was seeing skinny little Fahd for the first time. Fahd combined with Gordie's shot and Sam's strength made a formidable team, and the way Jenny was playing goal for them was equally astounding. Perhaps Muck was on to something.

Travis began watching his fellow Owls more closely. He was *scouting* them, even though he knew the four players on the ice almost as well as he knew himself.

There was something different about Sam. He began to focus on her, watching her even when she wasn't directly involved in the play, and it took him several minutes to realize what had changed.

Sam was running out of gas. She was gasping when the play left her. And she was coasting when she should have been skating.

It was as if she had no breath left.

Data found who he was looking for. The equipment manager was in charge of the California team, the Arrowhead Rangers. His name was Mr. Williamson – sort of a skinny Mr. Dillinger, with a full head of grey hair – and he was both very friendly and helpful.

"Funny you should bring that up," the Arrowhead equipment manager said when Data got around to asking his one important question. "We had the same thing happen here. I do my morning check – I like to sharpen all the kids' skates right away – and I pull out the bags and then restack them when I'm done. Same darned thing happened to us."

"What do you mean?" Data asked.

Mr. Williamson studied his nails as he thought about it. "We had one too many bags.

I figured one of the equipment guys from one of the other teams simply got mixed up and put it with our stuff. All those new tournament bags look exactly the same. So I just handed it back in."

"To who?"

"The organizers. They seemed pretty darned glad to get it, too."

"What number was it?"

"Huh?"

"The number – do you remember the number on the side?"

Mr. Williamson ran a hand through his thick hair. "Oh, that number. Yes, as a matter of fact I do, son."

"And it was?"

"Number 17. And you know what? We don't even have a 17 on the Rangers."

Data nodded and scribbled down the number on his notepad.

A number the Rangers didn't have. Just like the Panthers never had a number 44.

What did it all mean?

Travis could tell Fahd was starting to understand his new abilities in 3-on-3. With time running out on the Rangers, Fahd picked up the puck behind his own net, began coming out the left side, then twisted back to the right. The Rangers' quickest player swept around the net, chasing.

Fahd seemed so cool it was almost as if he was moving in slow motion. He tapped the puck back against the boards and turned again, just as the checker flew by and slashed his stick. It didn't even matter; the puck wasn't on Fahd's stick anyway.

He picked off his own pass and began to move up ice at such a leisurely pace it looked like he was on a public skating rink instead of in a high-pressure hockey tournament.

Andy slammed his stick hard, calling for a pass on the other side. A second Rangers checker tried to take the pass away, and went down on one knee as Fahd casually faked the pass to Andy. The checker lost his balance and twirled off into the boards.

Fahd kept the puck and moved directly to the net. He motioned as if to make a drop pass – the pass that was working so well for the Owls – and again a Rangers player went for it, lunging behind Fahd in the hopes of plucking the puck away from Sam, who was waiting to pick it up.

But again no pass. Fahd still had the puck, each of the Rangers now out of his zone and only the goaltender left. Fahd held on, waiting, moving slowly past the net until the Rangers' goalie flopped and kicked high with his pads in desperation.

Just as Travis had done against the Panthers, Fahd kept the puck and slowed even more, waiting while the goaltender drifted helplessly out of his own net, and then backhanded the puck high under the crossbar.

The stands exploded in appreciation. Travis could feel Mr. Dillinger's big hand pounding into his back. He could hear a wicked, high-pitched giggle as Nish pumped a fist for Fahd. He could see Sarah dancing with delight.

He felt good for Fahd. He felt, for a moment, as if he no longer knew Fahd. *Fahd, the star of the game?* Never before – but he sure was now.

15

THEY COULDN'T ALL CROWD INTO THE LITTLE dressing area, but they tried. Fahd was grinning from ear to ear. Andy was drained, his sweater off and his face still dripping with sweat. Sam was sitting with her helmet off and head stuck down between the tops of her shin pads, sucking for air. She looked pale and in pain.

Travis felt a finger poke in his back. He turned around quickly. It was Lars. "Data wants to see you," he said.

Travis backed out of the dressing room, the door muffling the sound of the happy players and their fans as it closed.

Data was sitting a little way down the corridor. He had his notepad on his knee, and looked extremely worried.

"What's up?" Travis asked.

"The snow globe that came out of that bag Nish carried back to the motel," Data said. "What became of it?"

Travis thought about it for a moment. "We put it in one of the drawers," he said. "Lars was going to exchange it, I think."

"Did he?"

Travis shook his head. "I don't think so," he said. "I think it's still there."

The worry lines on Data's face deepened. "I think we'd better go back to the motel as quickly as possible," he said.

Data explained on the way back. He had discovered that the confusion over Nish's bag wasn't an isolated incident. The Arrowhead Rangers' equipment man, Mr. Williamson, had also found a bag that didn't belong with his team's equipment. An extra bag, and a number on it that didn't connect to any of the Arrowhead players. A bag number 17, but no 17 on the team.

It seemed too much of a coincidence. Nish had picked up a bag intended for the Portland Panthers, and they had turned out not to have a number 44 in their lineup.

Data had borrowed a master team roster from Mr. Dillinger. It listed all the teams, all the players, and all the numbers. He couldn't find any other equipment managers, but he had been able to do a visual check of several of the other teams, counting their bags stacked up inside the locked storage areas. He was convinced several of the teams had one more bag than players on their roster. He hadn't been able to check if in each case there was a number that didn't fit on the team, but he had seen enough to become suspicious.

"Maybe they just threw in an extra bag for each team," suggested Nish. "A bag for the coach, or equipment manager – and extra equipment, in case somebody forgot something."

Data wasn't convinced. "Don't you think if that was the case they would have told the equipment managers?"

"What then?" Sarah asked.

"I don't know," Data said. "But I want to check out that snow globe Nish gave Lars."

"It's no good," Nish said, shaking his head. "We should have taken it back."

"That's just what I'm worried about," said Data.

They had almost reached the motel when Sam, who'd been hanging back with yet another of her cigarettes, caught up to the rest of the Owls and walked quickly, breathing hard, right through the centre of the gang.

Travis thought it was rude, and quite unlike Sam.

As she pushed through, her head held straight ahead, she whispered quickly out of the corner of her mouth: "*Don't anybody turn! There are three men following us!*"

"Impossible," said Nish, threatening to turn.

"*Don't look!*" Sam hissed again, her whisper almost becoming a shout. "*One's the guy Travis said was checking bags. The buzz-cut guy with the earring."*

Travis had to fight not to turn. He kept facing straight ahead, and the Owls, as a group, picked up the pace.

As they rounded a corner Travis allowed himself the quickest, tiniest peak back. He saw the man in the tinted glasses. His windbreaker was gone now – it was warm, the sun still out – and he was wearing a dark golf shirt. And two other men, both bulky, both in black T-shirts that showed off their beefy arms, were moving with him.

"What do we do?" asked Fahd.

"We get to the motel and find Muck," said Data. He had his wheelchair going full speed. Nish was pushing from behind, almost running.

"What do they want?" Sarah asked him.

"I think I know."

They made it to the motel, and once inside looked out through the glass door. The men had vanished.

"They weren't after us at all," Nish sighed in relief.

"Think again," advised Andy. "Look at the back of the parking lot."

The men were walking casually across the parking area, pretending to be moving towards their vehicle, but in fact they were turning to watch the kids and slipping in among the cars for cover.

"Get me to your room as fast as you can," Data ordered Nish.

"Somebody track down Muck or Mr. Dillinger," Travis called back. He was already fishing out his key to the room he shared with Nish and Lars.

Fahd and Andy split off to find the coach and the equipment manager. The motel seemed empty. It was such a fine day, everybody was probably out exploring. Travis had a sudden wish it was still raining, and that everyone was still in the motel. It was warm, but he shivered suddenly, worried that Muck and Mr. Dillinger wouldn't be around to help if the three men came after them.

But why? he wondered. Why would they come after a bunch of kids? What did they think they had?

Once Nish had pushed him into the room, Data began taking charge.

"The snow globe," he said. "Where is it?"

"It's in the bottom drawer," said Lars.

"It's no good," protested Nish. "It's broken, remember?"

"I'm not so sure," said Data.

Lars removed the box and opened it for the second time. The globe was still there. It hadn't been touched. The "snow" was still crystallized, meaning it was still broken. Travis couldn't see what the point was.

Data had Lars bring the globe to him. He set it in his lap and, with his good hand, began rolling it back and forth.

"See?" said Nish. "It's busted."

"I don't think so," said Data.

"What is it then?" Nish asked sarcastically. "*Fixed?*"

Data looked up at them all, his eyes filled with the same worry Travis had noted before. "It's cocaine."

"*Cocaine?*" Sarah and Sam said at once.

"*Drugs?*" Travis said.

"I think so," said Data. "We're going to have to call the police to be certain."

"I'm not so sure we've time," said Sam. She was looking out the window. "Those three guys are coming in the back way."

Travis looked out just in time to catch the third of the big-muscled men dip in the back entrance.

"What if they're coming after this?" Travis asked.

"If they get it," said Data, "there goes the evidence. It would just be our word against theirs."

"Like they're going to believe us!" said Nish.

Andy burst into the room, scaring them all. He seemed out of breath, frightened himself.

"Muck and Mr. Dillinger are out," he said. "There's nobody here."

"We better call the police," said Sarah.

"We better hide this," said Lars, picking up the snow globe.

"*Where?*" asked Nish. His voice cracked with fear.

"I don't know," said Lars. "Let's get it out of here. The window, maybe – those three thugs are inside the building."

Travis hurried into action. He was captain, after all. He was supposed to lead in moments of crisis. "I'll take it," he volunteered.

"I'm comin' with you!" Nish said at once.

"I'll come, too," said Sam.

Travis was already half out the window. Nish followed, then Sam.

Lars leaned out with the snow globe and passed it into Travis's outstretched hands.

He took it carefully, afraid of dropping it and breaking it. He cradled it like a baby against his chest.

"*Someone better be calling the police!*" Sam called up.

"*Sarah's already on the phone!*" Lars shouted down. "*Just get it out of here until they get here!*"

16

THEY RAN ACROSS THE LAWN AND OUT INTO THE motel parking lot. Travis looked in several different directions, suddenly unsure of where to run.

Nish came to his rescue. "*This way!*" he shouted. "*I know where it goes!*"

With Nish leading, the three Screech Owls began running as fast as they could. Nish moved quickly, puffing loudly but running well. He was already sweating. Sam covered the ground as fast as she moved on the ice, seeming to eat up the distance. Travis brought up the rear, finding it difficult to run as quickly as the others without his arms free. But he was holding the evidence, and had no intention of dropping it or leaving it or, worst of all, giving it up.

He heard Nish's voice, but at first he wasn't sure it was Nish. It sounded like a trapped animal, a squeal more than a voice, and filled with sudden terror.

"*They're coming!*"

Out of the corner of his eye Travis could see two burly figures moving out of the side door of the motel and into the parking lot. One pointed – *at him!* – and they began running in the Owls' direction.

"M-M-MOOOOOVE IT!" Travis found himself screaming.

The men were giving chase, the buzz-cut guy and one of the two muscle men. The third must have still been back in the motel, checking the rooms.

Nish was in full flight now, tearing down the streets past the university buildings, headed towards a dark, green park at the far end. Travis didn't know what to think. Perhaps they could lose the men more easily in a park. But then, if they did get caught, who would be there to help them?

There was no time for debate. They made for the park.

Travis could feel his chest burning. His breath seemed on fire as it jumped from his lungs. He was sweating, his heart pounding. Nish's face was beet red, his mouth wide open, and sweat danced in drops off his cheeks and forehead. Sam was breathing terribly, but still seemed strong.

Sam looked back at Travis. "*Here!*" she puffed, reaching out with both hands. "*I'll take it a bit!*"

Travis handed the snow globe to her gratefully. He felt instant energy, new speed as he gave it up, but the relief didn't last. Another dozen strides and his lungs were again on fire, his legs turning to rubber.

But he was doing better than Sam. She was suddenly falling back, crimson in the face, and gasping horribly for air. She stumbled once and nearly fell with the snow globe. Travis reached over and she handed it back. She seemed angry – but whether at him or herself, Travis couldn't tell.

Into the thick of the park the three Owls ran, their pounding running shoes snapping twigs and sending dirt flying. Branches stung their faces as they pushed through, hoping that around the next tree they would find an adult, a police-man – anyone who could help.

Sam was still slipping back. Her breathing seemed loud enough for all of them, deep rat-tling gasps that cut sharply through the silence of the bush they were invading.

Travis could hear the men crashing through the trees. They were cursing the branches and snapping them off as they elbowed deeper and deeper into the wooded park. Fortunately, the big men were slowing down in the thick bush. Had the branches not blocked them, they might already have reached Sam, who was steadily falling behind the two boys.

Did Nish really know where he was going? Travis wondered. He was acting like he knew, but Travis had known Nish to fake it a million times before. This was no time for bluffing.

Nish was up ahead, picking the path they would take. His head was spinning from side to side, a sure sign he was getting confused. Travis suddenly felt angry with Nish for bringing them there – but still, where else could they have gone? At least the men weren't gaining on them any more.

Sam suddenly stopped, gagging alarmingly as she tried to breathe. She leaned over and held one arm out, begging them to wait. She was beat, exhausted. It seemed she couldn't go on.

Up ahead, Nish stopped and spun on his heels, terror in his eyes.

"*We're trapped!*" he shouted back.

They had come to the ocean. They could go no further.

Travis could hear the men thrashing through the bush towards them.

"There's . . . b-beach . . . that . . . w-way!" Sam gasped, pointing.

They looked to their left. The woods gave way to open ground; beyond that was sand.

There were bodies in the distance.

Naked bodies!

Nish smiled. "I'm home!"

"You're dead!" Travis shouted angrily at him. This was no time to fool around.

Nish had led them to Wreck Beach, the nudist beach!

"*I can't run any more!*" Sam cried, her eyes filling with tears. She was puffing terribly, gasping for air.

"What'll we do?" Travis asked.

Nish had already decided – his shirt over his head, his shorts dropping over his sandals, his boxers down past his knees.

"*They'll never chase me there!*" he shouted.

He turned, buck naked, and yanked the snow globe out of the Travis's hands. Before they could say a word, he bolted out of the cover of the woods and onto the beach.

"GO FOR IT, NISH!" Sam called.

Travis couldn't believe it. He couldn't even speak. He could only stare at the back of the best friend he had in the world, Nish's barenaked cheeks churning as he hurtled, sand flying all about him, directly into the throng of early-season nude sunbathers.

Nish was wearing nothing but a snow globe, clutched so tight to his chest he looked like a football player heading for a touchdown.

"HEY!" a nasty, deep voice shouted. "STOP!"

A little distance away the two men had also broken clear of the woods. They couldn't see Travis and Sam in the cover of the branches, but they could plainly see Nish charging across the sand with the prize they were after.

They never even looked for Sam and Travis. They set off across the soft sand, sinking and stumbling with each step, two fully clothed men in dress shoes running and yelling into a crowd of peaceful nudists, most of whom were scattering with their towels and umbrellas to make way for the miniature nudist who was barrelling straight down the beach with what appeared to be a crystal ball in his arms. The stumbling men pushed on in pursuit, oblivious to the sudden rise of a police siren ahead at the far side of the beach.

Two police cars with flashing lights and sirens pulled off the hard ground and fishtailed onto the beach, throwing sand in every direction.

Nish never looked back. He kept on going towards the police cruiser, his legs a blur, his pink round body hunched protectively over the snow globe. And as the first policeman jumped out of the car, the naked young runaway blew right past him into the safety of the front seat.

The two men tried to turn back, but it was too late. They stumbled on the soft sand and went down, stumbled over each other again as they tried to get back on their feet. They fell back, cursing, as the police moved in on them with service revolvers drawn.

The two men threw up their hands in surrender.

Beaten by a naked twelve-year-old.

17

NISH AND FAHD CAME INTO THE MOTEL LOBBY, their arms filled with copies of the *Vancouver Sun* and the *Province*. Nish's photograph was the entire front page of one paper – "PEEWEE NUDIST FOILS DRUG CARTEL," blared the huge red headline – and his face beamed out in a smaller photo in the other paper, with a large map beside him showing the various places the RCMP had raided following the arrest of the thugs on Wreck Beach.

"The pictures are inaccurate," Nish announced as he handed out the newspapers to his teammates. "I shouldn't have any clothes on – but the stories are pretty good!"

The stories were astonishing. Travis and Sarah leaned over a copy of the *Sun* spread out on the floor, and raced each other to see who could come up with the most amazing detail.

"'PEEWEE TOURNAMENT PART OF INTERNATIONAL DRUG SCHEME,'" Travis read from one headline.

"'AQUARIUM COLLEAGUES STUNNED TO LEARN BIOLOGIST PART OF SMUGGLING RING,'" Sarah read, her voice sad rather than excited.

The story *was* sad. Exciting, obviously. Dangerous, obviously. But sad, too, for none of the Owls could take any pleasure in learning that Brad Cummings – the marine biologist who had been so kind to them during their visit to the Aquarium, the body they had found floating in the rolling seas off Victoria Harbour, the sweet, gentle man they all thought had been murdered because he tried to rescue a dolphin – had, in fact, been up to his neck in a very dangerous and criminal business.

"This is too much," Sarah said. And it was, for all of them. She was teary-eyed as she examined the newspapers. And Sam could only read a little bit before crunching up her newspaper and throwing it hard against the wall. She had then stomped out into the light rain, where she could now be seen, walking around the parking lot with her hands wrapped around her bare arms.

Travis read on, switching from one paper to the other, then back, trying to put it all together in a way that made sense.

But it was almost beyond sense. It seemed like they'd all been watching some fantastic, outrageous television show. But there was no remote you could push to turn it off, no happy ending, no feeling it was make-believe.

The mystery had been solved, but Brad and the dolphin were still dead.

Two other things were also certain. The mystery would never have begun to unravel if it hadn't been for Data's curiosity about the hockey bags. And the bad guys would never have been caught if Nish hadn't made that daring, naked dash across Wreck Beach with the broken snow globe in his arms. In fact, the snow globe wasn't broken, had never been broken. It had been exactly as Data had suspected, an ingenious way to smuggle cocaine.

If Travis had to take all these newspaper stories and reduce them to one simple explanation, the way they sometimes had to do in school, he would have written it down this way:

Smugglers had been using dolphins to get illegal drugs into the North American market. Cocaine was shipped up from South America, where it was manufactured. The fishing vessels carrying the drugs really were fishing along the Pacific Coast of the United States, but once they reached British Columbia the "fishermen" quickly became drug smugglers.

Canada is considered much easier to smuggle drugs into than the United States, so the smugglers chose the waters off Vancouver Island as the place to get the cocaine ashore. This is where the dolphins and Brad Cummings, a marine scientist with the Vancouver Aquarium, came in.

The story of Brad Cummings is unfortunate. He was, as friends and admirers believed, absolutely devoted to the welfare of dolphins. He was a leading expert in the training of dolphins and the study of their behaviour, and after many years of research he had developed a complex "language" of whistles that he used to communicate with them. To help finance an international campaign to outlaw the use of gill nets that have killed so many dolphins, Cummings had let himself become involved in helping the smugglers. He helped them land the drugs in return for tens of thousands of dollars, all of which he apparently turned over to various agencies devoted to animal welfare.

One dolphin, raised from infancy by Cummings, had been trained to carry water-proofed packages of drugs from the fishing vessels to a smaller boat closer to the shore, thereby avoiding detection by the Coast Guard and RCMP drug patrols.

According to an informant connected to the drug operations, shortly before his death Cummings came to believe he had been tricked by a smuggler and was owed ten thousand dollars. He instructed the dolphin to head out into open water with the drug payload instead of taking it directly to the drop-off point, and he refused to call it back until he'd received the money. The ransom trick failed. Cummings was murdered by the smugglers, who then used his special series of whistles to track down the dolphin, which was shot and the payload of drugs removed from its body.

This explains why the autopsies had discovered the man was killed some time before the dolphin. It also explains the markings on the dolphin, which had previously been mistaken for gill-net markings.

Once the drugs were taken to Vancouver, an elaborate scheme was devised to get the drugs across the border into the U.S. Shipment was to be arranged through the use of "mules" – innocent drug carriers – which in this case turned out to be peewee hockey players.

Teams from all over the United States and Canada were coming into Vancouver for a special 3-on-3 hockey tournament, and the smugglers arranged to have snow globes and new bags given out to each player participating. The smugglers then arranged to add an "extra" bag to each team, which would contain a snow globe with roughly $300,000 worth of high-grade cocaine in it.

Each team would play a single game just across the Canada–U.S. border at Bellingham,

Washington, and the organizers would transport the teams' equipment in a truck separate from the buses carrying the players. Once at the Bellingham rink, the "extra" bag containing the cocaine would be removed from the rest of the bags. The likelihood of border guards checking through the sweaty equipment bags of several dozen peewee hockey teams was remote indeed.

Had it not been for the work of Larry Ulmar, known to his teammates as "Data," the trick would never have been discovered. And had Wayne Nishikawa, better known as "Nish," not used his ingenuity to draw two of the smugglers to Wreck Beach, where they were immediately apprehended by police, the smugglers might have gotten away with their drugs *and* the murder of Brad Cummings.

Travis, on second thought, would change "murder" to "murders." He could not forget the poor innocent dolphin whose only crime was to obey instructions.

18

"WE BETTER FIND SAM," SARAH WHISPERED TO Travis. She looked worried. Travis nodded and folded up the newspaper he'd been reading. The stories were all beginning to repeat themselves anyway.

"She's in the parking lot," Travis said, but when they got outside they could see nothing. The parking lot was empty but for some swirling candy wrappers.

"I know where she'll be," said Sarah.

She led Travis out back where the garbage dumpster was, and there, as expected, was Sam, sitting on the curb, her legs folded in front of her. Her head was down. She was staring, almost as if hypnotized, at a dried leaf she was holding in one hand. Beneath it, in her other hand, she held a cigarette lighter, the flame licking upward towards the bottom of the leaf. The leaf began folding in on itself, almost as if panic had somehow struck it, as first smoke and then orange flame licked up through the centre.

Neither Sarah nor Travis said a word. They waited. And for a while it seemed Sam had no idea they were there.

Sam shook the leaf until it was nothing more than a stem and some black, curled char. She clicked off the flame, dropped the burned leaf onto the pavement, and getting up she tossed the lighter into the dumpster. She turned and looked at the other two. Her eyes were red. Possibly from the smoke of the leaf, but probably, thought Travis, from something else.

Sam looked a bit sheepish.

"The cigarettes are already in there," she said, nodding at the dumpster. "I've had my last smoke – I almost got us caught . . ."

Sarah looked perplexed, but Travis understood. Sam was looking straight into his eyes, as if searching for a signal – but what kind? Forgiveness? Blame? Travis could not blame her. Sam had helped as best she could. She had run for it with Travis and Nish when the easy thing to do would have been to stay in the motel and wait for the police. She had carried the snow globe when Travis had faltered. She had simply run out of gas, just like in the hockey game.

Travis smiled a smile that made words unnecessary. And from the look in Sam's eyes and her shaky smile in return, it was much appreciated.

Sarah, ever wise, asking for no explanation, also smiled at Sam.

Sam caught Travis off guard with a huge hug. For a moment it was he who had trouble breathing. Then Sam broke it off and hugged Sarah, who hugged her back.

"I wasn't a very good smoker anyway," Sam said, half laughing, half crying, "was I?"

"No, you weren't," agreed Sarah, also laughing.

All three turned at a sudden voice, calling out from the front corner of the motel. It was Fahd. He'd come looking for them.

"*Muck wants to talk to us all together!*"

⬤

"The tournament goes ahead," said Muck.

He was standing in the centre of the little motel lobby, turning as he spoke to the Screech Owls and the handful of parents who had come out to Vancouver with the team.

"I just got off the phone, and it's still a go," he continued. "The city has taken over and wants to ensure that the original intent comes off. Every team has agreed to a new format that will shorten things up.

"We're not playing any games in Bellingham. We're going directly to the finals. They did some kind of calculation to work out where each team stood, and for us it means some good news, some bad."

Muck pulled a sheet of motel stationery out of his pocket. He unfolded it, turned it around, and stared hard, trying to make out the scribbles he'd made in pencil.

"Dmitri?" he said slowly, looking up in search of the Owls' quickest skater. Dmitri raised his hand from the chair he was sitting in. "Your team's out, I'm afraid. Means nothing, okay? Just the way they juggled things around so they could wind this thing up fast."

Dmitri looked over at his teammates, Andy and Lars. Out because of a single loss. All they could do was shrug. It didn't seem fair – but who knew how they'd calculated which teams would continue? Some of the teams had played only two rounds of the 3-on-3, others had played as many as four.

"Liz, Derek, Willie?" Muck read out.

The three raised their hands.

"You're in the Rockies finals, okay? Game's in an hour, so you better go get your stuff together."

The lucky team whooped and high-fived their way out of the lobby.

Muck kept turning the paper one way, then the other, squinting hard as he tried to read his own terrible handwriting.

"Simon?" he said.

Simon Milliken raised his hand. Simon's teammates, Jesse and Wilson, moved closer.

Muck looked up. "Sorry, boys. Don't take it personally, though. Two wins and a tie, you should expect to go on. They must have just flipped a coin on some of these final match-ups."

The three looked stunned. They hadn't lost a single game. They'd played as well as they possibly could. Jesse slammed his fist into an open hand, Wilson dropped into an open chair, sighing.

Muck kept fiddling with his paper. He looked up a couple of times, peering about the room as if in search of someone who could help.

But there were only the two teams left. Sarah's team, with Travis and Nish, playing in the Elite Division, and Sam's team, with Fahd and Gordie, playing in the Canucks Division.

Travis's heart sank. Muck was just stalling. He hadn't the nerve to tell them they were out of the tournament, that the most fun Travis Lindsay had ever had in a pair of skates was about to come to an unexpected end.

"Sarah, Travis, Nishikawa?" Muck read.

"Yes," Travis said, speaking as captain.

But Muck didn't even acknowledge him. He read on: "Sam, Fahd, Gordie?"

"Here," said Sam. "Just put us out of our misery."

A slight grin flicked at the corners of Muck's mouth. He folded the paper and tucked it back

19

"THIS IS EMBARRASSING!"

Nish was almost completely dressed – pants, shin pads, socks, even skates complete with tape around the tops – everything but his shoulder and elbow pads and sweater. He was sitting, but leaning forward over his knees, his face red from the strain. Or perhaps it was anguish, given the way he sounded.

"What's *your* problem?" Sarah demanded as she pulled her sweater over her head.

"We're the *Elite* Division," Nish moaned. "We're not supposed to be playing against *Fahhhhdddd*."

The way Nish said the name, it sounded as if Fahd had never held a hockey stick, never worn skates, never touched a puck. It sounded as if he had no feet, no hands, no brain.

"Fahd's excellent at 3-on-3," said Jeremy, who had played more games than any of the others, since he and Jenny were in goal for five "teams."

"It's *em-bar-rass-ing*," Nish howled, as if the mere thought were painful.

Sarah shook her head. "You're the last person on earth to decide what's '*em-bar-rass-ing*,' Mr. Wreck Beach."

Nish straightened up, looking hurt. "Hey, c'mon, *I'm* the one who solved the murder, aren't I?"

Travis was about to argue the point when the door opened and Muck came in, smiling. He'd been in a great mood since Liz and Derek and Willie won the Rockies Division championship in a close 5–4 game against the team from Boston. But it wasn't his usual smile. It was almost as if Muck was enjoying some little private joke.

"Ready to go?" Muck asked, and they shouted that they were.

Travis pulled his number 7 sweater over his head, quickly kissing the collar as it passed his lips. Now, if he could only hit the crossbar during warm-up, he might have a good game.

"It wouldn't be fair of me to give you any scouting report on the other team," Muck chuckled. "All I can say is they're Screech Owls. That's usually enough to make any team play their best, and that's the least I expect of you. Now go out there and have fun."

"Who's coaching us?" Nish asked.

Muck winked at Sarah and Travis. "Not me, thankfully. I got the team that listens to its coach."

"What's that supposed to mean?" Nish said, trying to look innocent.

"It means, Nishikawa, that your coach is Data. Why don't you surprise him by doing as you're told, for once."

And with that, Muck turned and left. Only Travis was in a position to see that Muck was laughing to himself, enjoying the moment.

Data didn't have much to tell them. With Mr. Dillinger's help, Data had settled his chair behind the bench, where he was able to talk to the Owls as they leaned over the boards, but in fact there was little for a coach to do in 3-on-3 hockey. No lines to change. No big breaks or time-outs or ways of mapping out plays. Nothing but a few early instructions and then a lot of loud encouragement.

"Keep your eye on Fahd," Data said. "He's pretty good at this."

"'Keep your eye on *Fahhhhddd*,'" Nish mimicked. "C'mon, Data, get with it. This is a hockey game, not a spelling bee."

Nish turned and skated away, laughing at his own stupid joke. Fahd was, in fact, a pretty good speller at school, but he was also a pretty dependable little hockey player and, in 3-on-3, a crafty playmaker.

Sarah and Travis touched gloves for luck and skated back towards the faceoff circle. It felt odd to be out on the ice with Screech Owls sweaters skating around on the other side. Fahd and Sam and Gordie and Jenny were opponents, not team-mates, and even though Travis knew each of them so well, even though he counted them among his best friends, they were a bit like strangers now, their personalities and talents unknown.

But still, he felt good. He'd kissed his sweater. He'd touched gloves with Sarah. He'd hit Jeremy's pads in exactly the right order – right pad, left pad, left pad, right pad, blocker. He'd even hit the crossbar. He was ready to play.

He couldn't, however, say the same for Nish, who seemed to be taking this game far too lightly. Perhaps all the publicity had gone to his head.

The puck dropped and there was no more time to think. From now on, for Travis, it would all be action and reaction.

Sarah won the drop easily from Gordie. She fired the puck back to Nish, who turned and began skating casually back towards Jeremy. Nish rounded the net, came out the other side, and lofted a high pass that slapped and bounced past centre. Travis raced for it, but Fahd beat him to the puck.

Travis turned sharply, almost jumping back in the opposite direction. Normally he would have had a check, but Fahd, moving so slowly, so surely with the puck, wasn't doing what Travis expected. Instead of driving towards Travis's net, Fahd turned and skated cross-ice to the far boards, and Travis flew by.

Fahd held the puck and deked past Sarah, then flipped a quick backhand to Gordie, who fired a hard slapper as soon as the puck came within range. The puck slammed hard into Jeremy's pads and bounced straight out into the slot. Sam, driving from the point, hammered the puck home.

Owls 1, Owls 0.

No – Fahd 1, Nish 0.

Ten minutes into the game, Fahd's side was up 4–2 and dominating play. Sarah was skating well, and Travis felt he was playing fine, but Nish seemed oddly out of it, as if he wasn't taking anything seriously.

"Let's get it going!" Travis said as he brushed past Nish just before a faceoff.

"Don't worry," Nish said. "I've got it completely under control."

Sarah scored a beauty on an end-to-end rush in which she pulled Jenny out and roofed a backhander Dmitri-style. Fahd scored on another slowed-down play. Nish scored on a deflection. Fahd scored on yet another slow-down. Nobody seemed able to read him.

The rink was loud. It was packed with Owls and parents, and their cheering and yelling bounced off the ceiling and walls to combine into one great roar. Travis was sure he could pick out Lars's shouts at one point, and he thought he heard his own name being called, as well.

Lars would be shouting instructions. *Pass to open space. Use your body to open up holes for the others. Don't be afraid to slow things down.* Travis was trying them all, but it wasn't working.

Sam picked up the puck behind her own net and used the angle to beat Sarah's forecheck. She roared up over centre. Travis left her to Nish and concentrated on Gordie, trying to make sure Gordie wouldn't have space to get a good shot away.

Sam came straight at Nish. He was backing up, his hips working fast, and he was staring right at her. Perfect: just the way Muck taught. One-on-one, ignore the puck, play the man – or in this case, the woman.

Sam shifted the puck out on her stick, teasing.

Nish went for it, trying to poke it away, but Sam tucked the puck back in, and slipped it between his skates and out the other side.

Using her momentum she beat him on the inside, and looped around into the clear, scooping up the puck she'd just slipped through.

Nish turned the other way, sweeping his stick across the ice as he fell.

But it was too late. Sam was clear. She moved to her backhand, delayed, waited with the patience of Fahd, and then drilled a backhand high and so hard that it blew the water bottle off the top of the net.

The rink erupted in cheers. It had been a sweet enough play on its own, but it was the move on Nish that had electrified the crowd.

"Kind of undressed you there, didn't I, big boy," Sam said as she skated back past Nish. "Too bad this is a hockey rink and not Wreck Beach."

Nish never said a word, but Travis could tell he was steaming. And he could hear Sam's breathing, shallow and hard. She'd just skated the length of the ice, and they were all tired, but her breathing was louder and quicker than the others.

As Sam's game began to slip, Nish suddenly took his play up another notch. He hadn't said a word in answer to Sam after her magnificent goal, but Travis knew his friend well enough to know that his beet-red face was a sign Nish was ready to get serious.

Travis caught Muck's expression just before the faceoff. Muck was coaching from the other side, but he, too, had seen the change come over Nish. Usually Muck tried to provoke this in Nish to get him into a game, but now Sam had done it for him. Travis decided that Muck would probably be pleased. He wanted all the Owls to play well, even if it was against him. And getting Wayne Nishikawa to play the best hockey he could was something Muck counted among his greatest, if most difficult, achievements.

In the second half, Nish was like a whole new player. He was suddenly faster, smarter, slicker. He checked better. He passed better. He shot better.

Nish scored first on an end-to-end rush when he deked past Sam in a play almost identical to the one she had scored on. Nish scored on a terrific blast from the point after Sarah set him up and used her body to block Sam from getting to him. Nish scored on a two-on-one where Travis kept the puck for a long delay then slid a back pass to him for a hard, high one-timer.

They played, back and forth, for the full two periods of straight time, and when the horn finally blew the score was Owls 9, Owls 9.

It didn't matter which side was Fahd's, which side Nish's. The two teams were tied.

20

"WHAT HAPPENS NOW?" NISH AŞKED DATA AS they gathered at the bench to catch their breath and take in some water.

"Shoot-out," said Data.

"Who shoots?" Nish asked, expecting it would be him.

"Everyone," Data said. "Three shots – and if it's still tied, then it's one after another until one team goes ahead."

Nish scored. Travis scored. Sarah hit the post. Fahd scored. Sam scored. Jeremy caught Gordie's hard wrist shot.

Owls 11, Owls 11.

"What *now*?" Sarah asked when they returned to the bench. Nish was spraying water directly into his face.

"We pick a single shooter," said Data.

"Who?" Travis asked.

Data seemed reluctant to say.

"I've got to go with Nish," he said finally.

Nish shook his head. "Like there was ever any other choice."

Sarah turned to Travis, her eyebrows raised. "Is it ever okay to cheer for the other side?" she asked.

Travis just laughed. There was no answer for that. There was no explaining Nish.

The other side chose Sam. It caught Travis by surprise, because Fahd had played such a great tournament, but Sam was the better regular hockey player and had the good shot.

Sam was first. She went in fast, braked suddenly and slipped the puck through Jeremy's five hole.

Nish went second. He flew up and blasted a slapshot that went in under Jenny's arm.

Owls 12, Owls 12.

Sam went again, and scored again, this time on a pretty play where she deked left and scored from the right side, one-handed.

"It's all up to you," Data said to Nish.

"I know."

Nish picked up the puck at centre, moved slowly, then began cutting for the net. He faked and held, and Jenny moved with him, ready to stack her pads. He held still, waiting for the net to open, but Jenny held her position, drifting with him.

She'd obviously been studying Fahd's play. She was just as patient, just as determined.

Nish ran out of space. He had to shoot. He tried to lift it over her pads, but it was too late and the puck rang off the outside of the goal post and bounced harmlessly away.

Fahd's Owls had won the 3-on-3 tournament!

The rink erupted, as much in relief as in excitement. It had been an odd feeling, with everyone cheering for the Screech Owls and determined to be happy no matter what the score.

It had been a wonderful game. It had been a difficult tournament. It had been a terrible experience at times. But now, with the murders solved, with the tournament completed, and with the Screech Owls both champions *and* runners-up, life was returning to normal.

Finally.

The organizers came onto the ice for the presentation. There were gold medals for the winners and silver for the runners-up.

Then they announced the tournament MVP, and to no one's surprise, it went to Sam.

A woman came out carrying a square, silver-covered box and began to open it.

"*Hey*," called Nish. "*Maybe it's a snow globe!*"

"Get a life!" snapped Sarah, standing beside him.

But it was not a snow globe. Slowly the woman drew the trophy from the box.

It was a beautiful West Coast native wood carving.

Of a dolphin.

Sam burst into tears as she accepted it. She held it tight with one arm and threw the other around the woman, hugging hard.

The smiling organizers took it for tears of joy.

Everyone else in the rink knew that was only part of the story.

THE END

Sudden Death in New York City

Nish has done some crazy things before – but nothing to match this! At midnight on New Year's Eve he is planning to "moon" the entire world!

The Screech Owls have come to New York City for the year-end Big Apple Peewee Tournament. They'll be playing in Madison Square Garden, home of the New York Rangers, and on New Year's Eve they are going to Times Square for the "Biggest Party in History." The countdown to midnight will be broadcast on the largest TV screen ever built and beamed around the world by satellite. But Nish and Data figure out that with just a laptop computer and video camera they can interrupt the show – and Nish will have pulled off the most outrageous stunt ever.

Travis, Sarah, and the rest of the Owls have heard it all before. They are far more interested in the tournament and exploring the most exciting city on Earth. But no one anticipated just how exciting New York can be. A secret organization plans to disrupt the New Year's celebration in a more dramatic way than even Nish could have imagined. The countdown has begun ... and if the Screech Owls don't do something in the few seconds left, tragedy will hit Times Square.

THE SCREECH OWLS SERIES